THE MYSTERIOUS RECEDING SEAS

THE MYSTERIOUS RECEDING SEAS

Richard Guy

Copyright @ 2005 by Richard Guy

Library of Congress 2004097912

ISBN: 978-1-4134-3991-5

Editor   Constantina Tsetsos
Cover Illustration   Jason Guy
Graphics   Richard O, Gilvy

All rights reserved. No part of this book may be reproduced or transmitted in any form or by any means, electronic or mechanical, including photocopying, recording, or by any information storage and retrieval system, without permission in writing from the copyright owner.

This is a work of non fiction, Names, characters, places and incidents either are the product of the author's imagination or are used fictitiously, and any resemblance to any actual persons, living or dead, events or locales is entirely coincidental.

This book is printed in the United States of America.

To order additional copies of this book, contact;

The Institute of the Expanding Earth,
www.widemargin2000.com

"Dedicated to the hope that Earth Expansion and the Receding Seas Phenomenon will be realized and accepted in my lifetime"

Index

ILLUSTRATIONS

Table of Earth Expansion; Rand McNally	13
Faults of North America	42
World Ocean Floors	43
The San Andreas Fault	44
Samaria, Mesopotamia	45
South America-Africa 150 Million Years ago	46
Location of Earliest Civilization	47
The High Plains: Home of the Dinosaurs	48
Inca Civilizations	49
Aztec and Mayan Map	50
Egypt	51
Chinese Civilizations	52
Mesopotamia	53
Indus Civilizations	54
Mesopotamia (Between the Rivers) Showing successive sea levels	55
Ancient Egypt Page	56

PHOTOS

Mount San Michel surrounded by sea	57
Mt San Michel, deserted by sea	58
St Michel Mount Castle Penzance	59
Author at Greenwich Meridian	60
Lampoc Earthquake Fault	61
Afar Fault	62
Tibet Fault	63

FOREWORD

Surveys across the face of the Earth are obsolete unless frequently updated. The Earth moves as it expands and the human factor is unable to detect the subtle changes. Changes are slow and almost imperceptible.

Are our seas receding? Richard Guy says yes and puts forward conclusive proof that our seas have been receding undetected for millions of years.

Successive generations fail to notice the phenomenon because the sea is always assumed to be at a constant level. This is not so states Richard Guy and he sets out compelling arguments to prove the point. Sea level, he says, is an illusion that still clouds our perception today. The deception continues because sea level does not exist.

Guy takes you to Ancient Mesopotamia, Rome, Troy, Ephesus, and Egypt to show where the seas were in those times. This book will not only convince you but, forever, change your perspective on the way our civilization developed.

Satellites are showing us that all points move around on the face of the earth.

With the development of GPS it is now possible to track the subtle shift of coordinates on the earth's surface... A recent article in the Wall Street Journal tells us of a disparity between the boundaries of Rhode Island and Connecticut. The difference was some sixty feet out from the surveys done 140 years ago by Lewis and Clarke. This example as shown up by GPS is one isolated boundary disparity. It, however, has a domino effect nationwide an ultimately worldwide. If one boundary is wrong then it follows that all boundaries successively are wrong.

GPS will, no doubt, reveal in time that sea boundaries recede creating more land above sea level. It will no doubt confirm what surveyors have known for a long time and that is that no piece of real estate is in its supposed location on the face of the earth.

Our Earth is supposed to be a static earth, i.e. of constant dimension, neither contracting nor expanding. All theories therefore are tailor made to suit an earth of constant dimension.

My theory simply stated, is that the Earth is expanding and as a result the seas are receding. That is what this book is about.

Earth Expansion and Receding Seas working in conjunction give us clues to how Ancient Civilizations developed and why they developed in the highest mountains on earth.

The Earth is in a constant state of flux and it has its own agenda. We the inhabitants are the unwitting passengers. If however we accept that the earth is expanding we will understand a lot more of how we developed as a civilization. It will solve a multitude of anomalies that haunt Geologists, Paleontologists, Archaeologists, Earth Scientists, Engineers, Surveyors and a host of other disciplines.

If we continue to deny the obvious, close our eyes and minds and look the other way we do a great disservice to scientific progress. We have to question old and outdated concepts and overturn them if necessary. We cannot go on stumbling in the dark when there is so much light to let in. We must seek for the truth. The earth is deceptive. It has deceived us all through the ages. We will have to start looking at mirror images of what we have been taught about the earth and her behavior. If we do this it will make all the difference between going along for the ride or being taken for a ride.

Everyday new discoveries are being made in space. We are able to observe the birth and death of stars billions of light years away. We land vehicles and laboratories on Mars and circle Jupiter with great accuracy. We break down the components of the human DNA and perform miracles in surgery. Yet we don't know that our planet is expanding and that our seas are receding.

Richard Guy 2009

CHAPTER 1

"The Mysterious Receding Seas"

This is a book about levels, all sorts of levels. First and foremost it is about sea levels. Second it is about the history of sea level. In the third place it is about sea level historically. We refer to land levels as topography. Topography on maps is indicated by contour lines. Contour lines indicate points of similar terrestrial elevation. This book is therefore about topography and the part it has played historically. It is about topography in ancient times and topography today. Sea level determines topography for the simple reason that all terrestrial elevations are taken from sea level. We will deal with sea levels in ancient times to show how sea levels have influenced our lives in the past I will show how sea level still influences our lives today without us being aware of these influences.

For instance we take the levels on our street for granted. We never give them a second thought although we negotiate them from the time we awaken and step out of our house till the time we retrace our steps home. Our lives are dictated by levels but we don't see these levels because as far as we are concerned they are invisible. We also take the levels in our very homes for granted. The bedroom level the living room level the split-level all these levels relate to sea level but we never see that relationship. The levels where we work are all taken for granted. We pursue our daily lives and livelihood totally unaware of the influences of levels on our terrestrial existence. We don't know and we don't care that every level on land relates to sea level. For instance. When we get out of bed and stand on the bedroom floor: that level is related directly to sea level. When we walk down a stair we are stepping closer to sea level. When we walk across our floor to the front door we are walking on a level that relates to sea level. When we step out of our front door again we step on a patio level that is related to sea level. We never however stop to think in the normal scheme of things the significance of these levels. Is it any wonder therefore that we are also unaware of sea levels around us. We live our lives totally unaware of the levels around us; the levels that impact on our daily lives. All the terrestrial levels around us are invisible as we walk all over them. If that is the case with land bound levels. How then can we be expected to notice sea levels? The sea is remote to most of us as we go about our daily lives. Our lack of awareness of land levels is one thing. The lack of awareness of sea levels is quite another matter. Some continental people live their entire lives and not see the sea. How does one who lives in the middle of a continent relate to the sea? The sea is something only seen in a movie or on a brief vacation to a beach. That is what most of the worlds population sees of the sea. We are, therefore, not cognizant of the fact that our lives are dictated by sea level. That is quite understandable. How could we be aware that civilization is profoundly influenced by sea levels? The sea bequeaths new land to us every day of every age throughout millions of years of the earth's evolution... The creation of this new land has accommodated the expansion of all ancient civilizations. Yet we live our lives missing this most important historical fact. How could this be? The answer is simply that we don't have the time to observe the subtleties of the earth's behavior and we certainly don't have time to watch what the sea is doing. This land has been bestowed to us for our use. We use this newly created land totally unaware that it did not exist generations before. Millions of people in the world have never seen the sea or the seashore. So it cannot be a natural assumption that these people can relate with this formation of new land. People who live on the sea are hardly aware that something is happening. They really don't know what. If you ask them for an explanation they will relate it in terms of occupation. The will tell you about their fish pots. They will tell you they have to keep dropping them out further because the water gets shallower. They will point out landmarks that were once on the sea and now are away from the sea. In one case a diving board was standing away from the sea in sand. The board used to be over the sea. These are the things that you will hear from seashore people.

They will not, however, relate these anomalies with the receding sea. They, like everyone else, accepts sea level as a constant.

There is no way of telling because we are also totally unaware of what took place before we were born. After birth we are not able to live long enough to make any noteworthy observations of the seas recession. We live for perhaps seventy years on the average too short a time to reach any valid conclusion. This is the main reason this anomaly has never been discovered before. We previously had no means of spanning the generation gap. I am happy to say, however, that as of this writing the generation gap has been spanned and exciting discoveries are emerging. The future will only bring more and more surprises as we will see. When real estate people say that the earth is not making anymore land they are so wrong. The earth is making new land every day of every year all around the world. We will see how we use this land for our own purposes not knowing or understanding the more profound implications. We could even imply that the emergence of land from the sea is mystical for lack of our understanding of the bigger picture.

Our minds are conditioned by what we are taught in school. Much of what we are taught is not necessarily true. Scientists, have, for hundreds of years, studied the earth and earth's behavioral patterns. They proceeded to base theories on these observations. Over a period of time some of these theories creep into general acceptance and eventually into school curricula. Because these theories have been touted for a number of years and finally accepted does not mean that they are necessarily true. Some of them are out dated and definitely needs scrutiny. The dangerous development that follows acceptance of spurious theories is that other scientists come along and build theories on those dubious theories. This compounds the error and leads us further and further away from the truth. I will deal with this later. We however must be prepared to strike out on our own voyage of discovery and challenge these outdated and erroneous theories. As you read on you will be taken on a very interesting pilgrimage: a voyage of discovery into the past.

It is only by researching the past that we can confront the present and arrive at valid conclusions. We have to break new ground in our thinking. Forget what we have been already taught and start thinking for ourselves. We have to unlearn what we have already learned and open our eyes to a new world of exciting revelations.

Remember that all that you have already been taught was conceived by someone else and it was not necessarily the truth. Would it not be exciting to come up with some earth shaking discovery: a discovery that had your name on it... Well here is your chance.

First of all open your eyes to new possibilities like a child and you will be amazed at the utter simplicity of what I am about to show you.

Israel Beer Josaphat was born in Kassel Germany on July 21st 1816. His Father was a Rabbi. He went to London as a young man: converted to Christianity and changed his name to Paul Julius Reuter. He established a financial news agency the first of its kind in Europe. He was always obsessed with getting the news to travel faster. In Europe he used carrier pigeons to carry news. they proved faster than the conventional horses. In 1851 he laid a cable across the English Channel to improve the speed of his news service to mainland Europe. He no longer had to rely on carrier pigeons. To further improve his service he extended the cable from Britain to Ireland. Ships coming from America would drop off canisters with the news items into the sea off the Irish coast. The canisters would be picked up from the sea and the news content sent on to London by cable. The news would arrive days ahead of the ship.

Julius Reuter formed the French American company and launched his attempt to span the Atlantic from North America to Ireland with a cable. The Cable was laid in 1859. It was not successful at first for there were several problems. Some of the problems had to do with the lack of relays in the line: electrical surge control and a host of other problems. The most trying problem, however, was that the cables kept snapping on the ocean floor.

An interesting aside to this piece of engineering history. One morning in 2008 while walking to a site visit at Grammacy Park in New York I saw a brass plaque posted on a mansion at number 1 Lexington Ave. The plaque tells that the planning for the Trans Atlantic Cable took place on those premises one hundred and fifty years ago.

Earth's expansion over the last 4,500 million years

Age	4500	3500	2800	6000	present
Size ratio	1.0	1.2	1.36	1.82	1.93
Radius in miles	2060	2500	2750	3750	3980

My Father had extensive engineering experience building railroads in various locations and environments. He told me a lot of engineering stories when I was a boy. He had worked on the Panama Canal from the inception to completion 1903 to 1913. There he learned to build railroads. He worked under many famous American railroad builders and learned the profession well. After he left Panama he was called on, this time on his own, to build Railroads in the jungle of Honduras, the mountains of Haiti and the plains of Cuba. He was finally appointed superintendent of the Cuban Railroad system.

My Father told me the story of the laying of the transatlantic cable. He spelled out all the details of the problems encountered. I was fascinated with this story as well as all the other engineering achievements he told me about.

The one problem that stuck in my mind and remained there for years to come: was this. He said that when the cables were laid they kept snapping. The snapping cables were a persistent problem throughout the fledgling years of the cable laying attempt.

At that time the sea floor was unknown territory and in some respects it still is. No one knew what the sea floor looked like. The general perception was that it was level and covered with sand. There was no logical reason for the cable to snap. Yet they kept snapping. Consultants were called in to provide answers. Large grapplers were designed to repair the cables. It was an expensive operation. Two ships had to go out to the Mid Atlantic and drag the sea floor which is one and a half miles deep. It is like searching for a needle in a haystack. The broken ends of the cables had to be grappled and brought to the surface. They were then brought on to the deck of the ships to be repaired. They were then dropped back into the ocean only to snap again.

It was a colossal expenditure to lay cables on the sea floor. To have the cables break was further expense as they had to be repaired again and again every time they broke. The repair operation was continuous and costly... These breakages occurring frequently, as they did, disturbed the investors. When the cable snapped communications were naturally suspended making investors unhappy.

Scientists were consulted as to the cause of the breaking cables. At that time, no one knew what the sea floor looked like.

The cable companies were plagued with the problem of cable breaks through all the years that followed.

When I asked my Father what caused the breakages he told me what the scientists deduced. "The cables were being broken by undersea Currents and Landslides" At that time I was only a boy but I remember thinking to myself. That reason does not sound plausible. I did not know what caused the breakages but I certainly didn't believe that that was the cause.

However, because the problem of breaking cables persisted years into the future the scientific explanation of undersea landslides and undersea turbidity currents became part of scientific lore from that time onward. So we will keep this in mind as we read on.

On the morning of November 15th 1957 at 3.30AM a Norweigan Freighter sailing from South Africa into the Mid Atlantic ran into an undersea mountain top, a seamount, as they are called. The ship was lost and the crew miraculously saved by another freighter who answered her distress call. Lloyds of London along with the worldwide maritime community decided that something had to be done. After thousands of years of maritime activity the sea floors had never been mapped. The problem was that there was no technology, up to that time, to do the job properly.

During the Second World War, however, sonar had been used and perfected. It was decided that side sweep sonar was to be used to initiate the first comprehensive sea floor mapping program that had even been attempted and the year 1957 was designated the International Geographical years and in that year the sea floor mapping would commence. Also planned for that year was another ambitious scientific Endeavour. Scientists would attempt to drill cores into the seafloor of the Mid-Atlantic to retrieve some of the oldest sediments on earth It was thought at the time, and logically so, that the deepest sediment on earth would be found at the bottom of the Mid Atlantic. As I mentioned before we were all ignorant of what the sea floor looked like. It was, therefore, most natural to assume, in the thinking of the times, that the sea floor held sediment that would tell of the origins of life on earth and perhaps the age of the earth. Hopes ran high in scientific circles awaiting the findings from this experiment.

In 1957 the sea floor mapping started in the Atlantic and continued into successive years. It was a long term program that would go one for years and in fact is still going on this many years later.

By 1959 the scientists were able to announce some exciting findings. They had discovered a range of mountains running in the middle of the Atlantic

Not only did they discover one range of mountains but there were two parallel ranges running one mile apart up and down the Mid Atlantic. The mountains crested out at 9000 feet with a chasm in between them similar in width to the Grand Canyon. This in itself was a major discovery and the scientists realized that it defied any preconceived notions we ever had of the sea floor. But many more surprises were to come.

The discovery of the parallel mountain chain solved a major mystery. For the very first time the scientific world realized the true cause of the snapping cables. They finally discovered why the cables snapped and kept snapping. What had been happening was that the cables laid on the sea floor had to span the mile wide canyon. These cables were designed to sit snugly on the sea floor of sand which was all in the imagination back then. The fact is that they were never designed to span ten feet much less a mile. They were not designed like cables on a suspension bridge to take all the imposed loads and in addition their own weight. The cables snapped because they were overstressed. The weight of the water from the ocean above them would have snapped them over any small span. At that depth of one and a half miles the pressure on a spanning cable would have been tremendous.

So after all these years of erroneous theories the truth eventuality came to light. There were never any Turbidity Currents and Undersea landslides. Yet for 100 years we all believed what the scientists told us. Now we knew the truth and all those scientists are long gone. Their theory however lived on for 100 years and was accepted. There is a lesson here.

The project to take samples of the sediment on the sea floor also had its fair share of surprises. The first core samples were taken from the floor of the Atlantic in between the two parallel mountain ranges which they had recently discovered. Scientists were amazed. They had expected to find thick sediment that would tell them the history of the earth. Instead, and much to their surprise, they found that the core samples revealed new sea floor. They subsequently discovered that the area between the mountain ranges was oozing new lava from the earth's interior. This lava was pushing outward east and west. The action was not only pushing the mountain ranges further apart but was also pushing North America further from Europe. Later they were to find that the progressive outward flow of lava was separating Europe from North America by about six feet every sixty years. Did this mean that the earth was expanding? That was one possibility. However, we are taught that the earth is static which means that it does not expand.

Arising from this discovery scientists of the static earth were faced with a dilemma. If in fact the Atlantic was expanding then the Pacific had to be contracting. This would make the static earth remain static. This was the thinking at the time and this prevailed for some years until it was proven that the Pacific was also expanding. So where does that leave the static earth theorists. Well if both the Atlantic and Pacific were expanding then the continents shelves must be sub ducting. And so the Seduction theory came into being. All these theories to justify an earth that did not expand. After many years the seduction theory is being questioned for its many imponderables. There is no viable proof. So here we are at a crossroads where scientists are fighting to keep the earth static when all indications are to the contrary. The earth definitely appears to be expanding. So let's move on.

CHAPTER 2

Julius Reuter took a giant leap when he laid the cable across the Atlantic. It took 100 years to find out why his cables snapped. The reason was the expansion of the Atlantic.

In 1851 when he laid his first cable across the English Channel nobody warned him that the British Isles were separating from Europe. The truth is that no one knew that at the time. Twenty four million years before Julius Reuter would not have had the problem of spanning the English Channel. No cable would have been necessary because the British Isle was welded to Europe at that time. Over the last twenty four million years the British Isle has separated form Europe and is gradually moving away.

I stressed in the beginning of the book that in order for us to debate the future of sea level recession or the existence of the phenomena we have to go back into ancient History. We have to look at life in ancient times from a sea level perspective.

We will start by looking at ancient Rome and what it has to show us about sea level.

There are several aspects of Rome that I personally find appealing. Is is a fair city with a magnificent historic past and enthralling present day appeal. I always yearned to go to Rome from I was a boy. I attended a Jesuit College and did five years of Latin. At the end of five years we were able to converse in Latin. We studied Virgil and the Anneid and were ardent Latin scholars. I read the epic narrative poem by Macaulay. "The Lays of Ancient Rome" which I discovered in my Fathers collection of books in the small Family library. I was transported by the colorful narrative poetry back to ancient Rome. The poem related the saga of a Roman Horatio Cocles. It told how he held the bridge to Rome against an army of ten thousand led by the infamous Lars Persona. Horatio and two of his friends in Rome volunteered to hold the bridge against the invading army while the other consuls of Rome demolished the bridge. The idea was that if they held the bridge long enough they would deprive the invading army of access to Rome. The River Tiber had a strong current which no army could cross. At that time Rome was a small city and the Subliceus Bridge was the only access to the City. The bridge was constructed of wood and could be easily chopped down with axes. Once Horatio and his friends went across the bridge to face the on coming army the consuls started chopping on the bridge to bring it down. The idea was that they would call back the three brave Romans before the bridge fell.

Horatio and his embattled friends held the bridge bravely and eventually at a signal from the Consul his two friends ran back across. However as Horatio was about to cross the bridge it collapsed leaving him alone to face the arrayed army. The army up to that time had been frustrated by the dauntless three. Now they had Horatio at their mercy. All the men in the vanguard of the army started jeering Horatio for they were certainly going to kill him. Horatio ignored them and placed his sword on his back: said a prayer to the Tiber and plunged headlong in the foaming river. Horatio was wounded and bleeding from a gash in his thigh. He was heavy with the added weight of armor and sword. For what seemed an eternity his head did not come up above the water but when it did both the Romans and the opposing army cheered the heroism of Horatio. He was welcomed as the hero by the Romans and conferred with many honor.

This story fascinated me and I always longed to go to Rome to see the mighty Tiber and visit the bridge which Horatio held so well. The opportunity came while I was a student in London. I got married and we decided that we would go on the continent for our honeymoon. We crossed the English Channel to Ostend: drove through Belgium into France and then into Germany and Switzerland. We drove through the Alps down into Italy. I wanted to save Rome for the last so we went to Venice and then to Rome. I was very excited getting into Rome. I was so excited at the prospect of seeing the mighty River Tiber. As we entered Rome I stopped on the first Bridge: parked the car and ran to the rails to see the river. I was shocked into silence for there was no river. There below the bridge was a vast area of sand and a little trickle of polluted water running in serpentine fashion through the sand. I was very disappointed and it took me sometime to overcome the shock of where all the river water had gone? It was fortunate that we had a lot to see in Rome so I spent the time sightseeing but all the while my mind was dwelling on the loss of the River. My thoughts lingered on the River. How could a river disappear? Among the many interesting events in Rome we went to visit an old school friend at the Vatican. My friend had attended college with me and had gone on to study for the priesthood in the Vatican Seminary in Rome. He had become quite a linguist in seven years mastering seven languages. I discussed the Tiber with him and he too commented on the anomaly. He too had read "The Lays of Ancient Rome." He encouraged me to go to Ostia. Ostia is fourteen miles from Rome. He told me that Ostia was "Portus Romanus", the Roman Port, in ancient times but no longer because it had silted up. My wife and I set out for Ostia and I was very glad that I did.

Ostia was the major Port to Rome during the time of the Punic Wars i.e. the wars with Carthage. All the grain and other commodities coming to Rome were brought into Ostia. From Ostia they were transshipped up the Tiber on barges to Rome. The Barges were pulled upriver by horses plodding along the Tiber embankments. At that time the river flowed full and the water at Ostia was deep enough to accommodate ships that drew six feet of water. At one period a canal was constructed to the Tiber from the harbor. It is important to mention also that at the time when Ostia served as the Port for Rome it was located on the estuary of the Tiber. Ostia like many ports around the Mediterranean made salt for their domestic use and also as a currency. In Latin the word for salt is Sal-Salis. The Roman legions were paid in salt for it was a precious commodity. The English word "Salary" comes down to us from that practice. The word Soldier also derives from the Latin words "Sal Dare" to give salt. The word Salient also comes down to us as something outstanding.

At Ostia salt reservoirs, or pans as they were called, were constructed on the shoreline. When the sea came in at high tide it flooded the salt pans, and as the tide receded they closed the sluice gates capturing the sea water in the pans. The sun did the rest of the work. As the water evaporated it left saline slurry on the bottom of the pans. This slurry was placed in large vats and the remaining water boiled away until only the pure salt remained. Many ports around the Mediterranean made salt in the same fashion. When the Romans eventually sacked Carthage and burned it to the ground the soldiers were ordered to take the salt from the salt pans of Carthage and cover the earth surrounding the city so that nothing could grow there again.

When the commodities from Ostia were barged up to Rome they were stored in large warehouses constructed on the banks of the Tiber... The warehouses on the Tiber were rediscovered just sixty years ago. When you stand on the docks and observe the height of the docks where the cargo was stacked you have to wonder where thirty feet of water in the river has gone. You can see clearly where thirty feet of river water is missing. Where had the River gone?

The other anomaly is that the level of the docks in relation to the River height back in those times relates well with the salt reservoirs at sea level at Ostia at that time. So where has all the water gone? Another puzzle is that Rome was founded originally on seven hills and all around those hills were malarial swamps. History tells us that the legions that went from Rome and returned marched through coastal marshlands. Over the two thousand years since then the marshes have all disappeared from the coast but that is not all. The salt pans at Ostia which were once at sea level are now twenty feet above sea level. In addition Ostia, which was once on the sea at the estuary of the Tiber, is now three miles from the sea. The salt pans are now used as fresh water reservoirs to irrigate all the agricultural land that run down to the sea, which lands were incidentally under the sea at Ostia. After a time the harbor at Ostia started getting shallower. Successive Emperors tried to keep the harbor open by dredging. The Emperor Trajan realized the strategic importance of keeping Ostia open. He was aware however that he was working against a relentless force. The sea was receding and nothing could be done about it. Ostia lost the fight and its harbor to as a result. The receding sea had won. Today like yesterday at the time of Trajan and the Punic wars we are still not aware of this relentless force. We have not realized that our seas are receding. The method of dredging in ancient times was no match for this mysterious force. It is therefore safe to say that the only improvements we have made over the last 2200 years since Carthage are improvements in dredging equipment.

All the harbors around the Mediterranean have had to construct new harbor facilities as the sea recedes making their harbors shallow. Most harbors around the world are kept open by dredging. Dredging is continuous and also costly but it has to be done to keep busy ports open. What is interesting is the fact that harbor authorities around the world keep dredging because they have no choice. They are of the opinion that the harbor is silting up. They are totally unaware of the bigger picture. They don't know that they are fighting against a global phenomenon. They are really fighting against declining sea levels caused by the seas recession. So they keep dredging in total ignorance. It is a continuous process.

New York Harbor has been dredging for years. All the channels have to be kept open as ships get bigger and bigger demanding greater draughts. Now for the first time New York Port Authority will have to start blasting bedrock to maintain the depth they demanded in the future. Why is all this dredging necessary if sea level has remained the same through the ages?

When St Paul the Apostle traveled around the Mediterranean spreading the Gospel he made successive visits at Ephesus. He even lived there for three years on one occasion. Ephesus had a spacious harbor and Paul sailed in several times on his missionary journeys. Sometime in the first century AD the harbor started silting up, I use this term because that is the general interpretation, The Roman Emperor tried to keep the harbor open by dredging but slowly Ephesus lost it's harbor. Today Two Thousand years later Ephesus is six miles inland away from the sea.

When Helen ran off with the handsome Paris to Troy it started the Trojan War. Menelaus, her incensed husband, assembled a fleet of a thousand ships to go to Troy and lay siege to the city to reclaim his unfaithful wife. The fleet assembled at Mycenae in Greece and sailed for Troy which was at the mouth of the Dardanelles. Troy had a large crescent shaped harbor which easily accommodated the invading armada. The siege of the city continued for ten years. Eventually the Greeks used the ploy of the Wooden Horse and finally sacked Troy and reclaimed Helen. It was reported that when Menelaus finally seized Helen. He drew his sword to slay her. Helen quite aware of her attributes bared her breasts to him. He was so smitten by her beauty that he sheathed his sword and forgave her. That act of forgiveness tells us how long ago that must have been.

Today the ruins of the City of Troy are six miles inland. Its ancient Harbor is now agricultural land running down to the sea miles away...

The City of Mycenae in Greece from where the fleet sailed to Troy is also six miles inland today. The City of Ephesus which is approximately two hundred miles from Troy on the Aegean Sea is also six miles inland. This recession of the sea is obvious all around the Aegean, the Adriatic and Mediterranean Seas.

Ravenna in the time of the Roman Empire was a naval harbor. The early settlement was built in the marshes. The first structures built there were stilted houses that sat over the malarial swamps. Again I must point out that the entire coast of all these countries around the Aegean, Adriatic and Mediterranean Seas were all marshlands. Over the last two thousand years all the marsh lands have disappeared with the receding seas. The sea maintains the coastal marshlands: as the sea recede the marshlands dry up and disappear. This phenomenon happens around the world. Today Ravenna is also six miles inland. It is on the Adriatic Sea. I have now shown you examples of the seas recession on the Mediterranean Sea in the Case of Rome. I have shown you examples of the recession on the Aegean Sea in the cases of Mycenae, Troy and Ephesus. And now I have shown you an example of the seas recession on the Adriatic Sea. All these seas are interconnected with the Mediterranean and the greater Atlantic at large. You must keep that in mind as you read on. Later I will show you examples of receding seas in both hemispheres.

History holds the secret to receding seas so we have to go back to times long ago. We have to use history and historical places to cast light on the receding seas.

Benomini Gigli was a great Tenor on the world stage after Enrico Coruso. In 1956 my wife and I attended his farewell concert at the Royal Albert Hall in London. Gigli was retiring from the stage and returning to his native land Italy. While he thanked the audience that night for their support through the years he mentioned something very interesting. It might not have resonated with many people in his audience but it certainly did with me. He said that he was from the small town of Recanati on the Adriatic Coast of Italy. He went on to say that his city had been a seaport in times gone by but today was six miles inland. It is funny how the mention of such a tiny morsel of information can start a lifelong quest. Benomini Gigli returned to Recanati and died a year later in 1957.

At that concert I ran into an old school friend who was then the Reuter correspondent in Rome. After the concert we spoke at some length and I mentioned what Gigli had said about Recanati. My friend had been to the town and confirmed that it was true. He went on to say that all the coastal cities along the Adriatic that were once on the sea were now miles inland. That simple conversation in 1956 changed my life. I was off on a lifelong quest and the most exciting part of my life. As the years progressed I accumulated more and more facts about historic places and their relationship with the sea.

Biblical stories also provide a lot of research material as I will show. The Exodus is one famous example in Biblical history which comes to mind. The Bible tells us that the Israelites were finally given permission by Pharaoh to leave Egypt. They gathered at Ramsees and filed towards Pithom after which they crossed the Red Sea nearby. History tells us that these two Cities were built as store cities by Jewish Slave labor. These cities were an integral part of Jewish history and also the historic connection to the Exodus. To find them was critical.

Historical accounts tell us that both Ramsees and Pithom had ports: they were both on the sea. The problem however was that these two cities, so important to the Exodus Story were lost in antiquity. Archaeologists searched for years to find these cities without success. Because historical records told them that both cities had ports the archaeologists carried out their searches on the shores of the Mediterranean Sea. Their searches yielded no information throughout many years.

The city of Ramsees was not discovered by Archaeologists but by a farmer. The Farmer while ploughing his land hit a stone which was hidden below the surface of his field. When he examined the stone it had hieroglyphs on it. He called in the archaeologists who read the stone glyphs and declared to the world that they had discovered the ancient city of Ramsees. This was indeed a historic find. It was a direct link to the Exodus story and to the Pharaoh Ramsees 2. The most puzzling aspect of the discovery was that the city of Ramsees was six miles from the Mediterranean Sea. Remember we are still on the Mediterranean and all the other cities I have mentioned so far are all six miles inland.

The discovery of Ramsees was made in 1883. One hundred and twenty six years ago.

This time frame is a short interval in the eternal process of the seas recession. We also have to remember that most of this recession has taken place over thousand of years. How many thousands are your guess as well as mine? But we also have to remember that further back in history the seas were much higher. The further back we go the higher the sea levels get.

After the city of Ramsees was discovered it was much easier to find Pithom with the directions given in the Bible. The bible account states that they filed past Pithom and from there crossed the Red Sea. Puzzles still remained because remember that back in ancient times Pithom also had a harbor. Where had the harbor water gone? History also records that Ramsees 2 dug a canal from a branch of the Nile to Pithom to give him access to the Red Sea. The canal that Pharaoh dug was evident and it did terminate at Pithom. This showed that the historic account was true. Pithom was on the sea. Today historians tell us that the Israelites crossed the Red sea near to the town of Ismailia.

This introduces us to another phase of this historic drama.

Ferdinand Delesseps got permission from the Khedive of Egypt, Ismail to build the Suez Canal. The canal was completed in 1869. It was one hundred miles long. A new city Ismailia, named to honor the Khedive, was established midway along the canal. The city Ismailia is situated exactly in the middle of the Canal i.e. fifty miles from Port Suez on the Red Sea and 50 miles from Port Said on the Mediterranean Sea. Modern day historians tell us that the Israelites crossed the Red Sea near to Ismailia.

Coincidentally the ancient city of Pithom was discovered near to Ismailia in the middle of the Suez Canal. So the account of the Israelites passing Pithom and crossing the Red sea is accurate. The account, today, that they crossed near to Ismailia is also accurate.

However the puzzle still remains where is the Red Sea that once made Pithom a Harbor. The Red Sea is fifty miles away from Pithom today. At the time of the Exodus it was possible to sail from the Nile River via a canal to Pithom which allowed you access to the Red Sea.

The Suez Canal is a sea level canal. This simply means that you can sail on one sea level from the Red Sea to the Mediterranean Sea. There are no locks like in the Panama Canal.

In fact there is a slight difference in sea level between the Red Sea and the Mediterranean. The Red sea is slightly higher. Because of this there is a flow from the Red Sea to the Mediterranean Sea. It is nothing to be concerned about except for the environmental consequences which have been experienced over the years.

The sea levels all along the Canal, we have established, allows ships to sail right through unobstructed by locks. So when the Red Sea was at Pithom in antiquity the Mediterranean Sea must have also been at Pithom. It is quite plausible to assume that the two seas met at that mid point of the canal at Pithom. It is also quite plausible that both seas obeyed their respective tidal regimens and withdrew at times and clashed together at high tides. The Israelites labored in that area of Egypt and knew the area well. They must have been cognizant of the tidal movements of both seas. It is also quite plausible that they crossed at that location because they had all this information. I am not trying to rewrite history but just pointing out possibilities. At that time also the height of sea level gave Ramsees its harbor on the Mediterranean. In summation therefore it appears that Ramsees had it harbor on the Mediterranean Sea and Pithom had its harbor on the Red Sea. In closing this treatise of the Exodus I have to point out one more anomaly. Why did the Israelites leave the city of Ramsees to file in their thousands to cross at Pithom.? They were evidently walking along the shores of the Mediterranean to get to Pithom : the point where both seas clashed. You can draw your own conclusions.

Some years ago I went to Key West to visit Hemmingway's house... I was surprised to see that the Key West lighthouse was right across the road from his house. What was a lighthouse doing in the middle of a built up city? Of course I knew that the Lighthouse was built there years ago when the city had not yet grown. I also knew instinctively that the light house was built there when the sea was nearby. What had happened was obvious. The sea had receded leaving the lighthouse behind and the city grew up on the land deserted by the sea.

Fort Zachary Taylor is also in Key West. The fort was built during the civil war it was completed in 1868. The fort is a popular tourist attraction because it houses a large collection of old armory from the civil war period. On a visit to the fort there are brochures that show the fort out in the sea. It was built out in the sea so that the sea would act as a natural moat. It had one narrow causeway leading out to the Fort when it was constructed one hundred and forty years ago. Today Fort Zachary is part of the mainland and the sea is far gone.

Sometime in the fifties we were building an oil refinery in Milford Haven in Wales.

Oil Refineries are constructed mainly of steel. All the structural components are steel.

The refinery was being built right by the sea. On the site one morning I mentioned this to the foreman. It was just a passing observation. I said. "The sea air will play havoc with all this steelwork." Oh he said" Where we are building the refinery was once under the sea. In another hundred years the sea will be a mile away. That little snippet of information has always lingered in my mind.

Sometime in 2002 I was building some commercial buildings in Houston. The electrical contractors had dug a trench to run cables to one of the buildings. There were large chunks of black soil resting on the side of the excavation. That morning at a site meeting I mentioned to the Architect that the soil looked rich. I said. "I bet that that soil could grow anything it looks so fertile?" The architect reached down and took a clod of soil in his hand and crumbled it. He said. "Richard this soil is full of salt the sea just recently deserted these lands." It was then that I recalled that all the surrounding area was low-lying quite a distance away. I would never have related the distance with his use of the word recently.

The truth is that the sea recedes relatively quickly in some areas and not so in others.

There is an article in the New York Times May 17 2009 telling about the retreat of the sea in Juneau Alaska.

Here I paraphrase the article "Morgan DeBoer, a property owner, opened a nine-hole golf course at the mouth of Glacier Bay in 1998, on land that was underwater when his family first settled here 50 years ago.

"The highest tides of the year would come into what is now my Driving range area," Mr. DeBoer said.

Now, with the high-tide line receding even farther, he is Contemplating adding another nine holes.

"It just keeps rising," he said.

The geology is complex, but it boils down to this: Relieved of billions of tons of glacial weight, the land has risen much as a cushion regains its shape after someone gets up from a couch. The land is ascending so fast that the rising seas — a ubiquitous byproduct of global warming — cannot keep pace. As a result, the relative sea level is falling, at a rate "among the highest ever recorded," according to a 2007 report by a panel of experts convened by Mayor Bruce Botelho of Juneau.

The panel experts are using the Isostatic Rebound Theory to describe what is happening in Alaska. They use the cushion analogy. The Isostatic Rebound theory is flawed, and hence, erroneously portrays what is really taking place in Alaska as well as around the world.

Greenland and a few other places have experienced similar effects from widespread glacial melting that began more than 200 years ago, geologists say. But, they say, the effects are more noticeable in and near Juneau, where most glaciers are retreating 30 feet a year or more.

As a result, the region faces unusual environmental challenges. As the sea level falls relative to the land, water tables fall, too, and streams and wetlands dry out. Land is emerging from the water to replace the lost wetlands, shifting property boundaries and causing people to argue about who owns the acreage and how it should be used. And melt water carries the sediment scoured long ago by the glaciers to the coast, where it clouds the water and silts up once-navigable channels.

A few decades ago, large boats could sail regularly along Gastineau Channel between Downtown Juneau and Douglas Island, to Auke Bay, a port about 10 miles to the northwest. Today, much of the channel is exposed mudflat at low tide. "There is so much sediment coming in from the Mendenhall Glacier and the rivers — it has basically silted in," said Bruce Molnia, a geologist at the United States Geological Survey who studies Alaskan glaciers.

Already, people can wade across the channel at low tide — or race across it, as they do in the Mendenhall Mud Run. At low tide, the navigation buoys rest on mud.

Eventually, as the land rises and the channel silts up, Douglas Island will be linked to the mainland by dry land, said Earn Hood, a hydrologist at the University of Alaska Southeast and an author of the 2007 report, "Climate Change: Predicted Impacts on Juneau."

Isostatic Rebound, simply stated, assumes that sea level is static, i.e. never rises never falls. Global warming, states that as the Glaciers melt sea levels will rise. That is not what is reported in Juneau. In fact the opposite is taking place. The Glaciers are melting and the sea level is falling. It seems that in Juneau the reality is in direct conflict with what the Global Warming exponents forecast.

For over thirty years I have been saying that our seas are receding and as a result the land appears to rise. The land does not actually rise it is an illusion aided and abetted by the generally accepted mindset that sea level is a constant.

The sea level fall in Alaska should be noted and appreciated for what it is telling us. It is telling us that sea levels all over the world are receding because our planet is expanding. This is the point I have been making consistently for years. We have to wean ourselves away from the mean sea level concept and realize that sea level is receding constantly. We waste a lot of precious time and scientific discovery when we hold to the outdated concept of a sea level datum. I have stated over and again that sea level datum is a myth it does not exist. We really don't know sea level and we never will: because sea level is not level.

We must remember that we are the best arbiters of what we read and assimilate. We have to use our own minds to probe and determine what is acceptable and what is not. Global Warming forecasts strike terror when they say that seas will rise by twenty feet in fifty years.

Are we going to believe that? Another article in the New York Times May 14th 2009, Times Topics, relates the latest statement about Global Warming and sea level rise. Here I quote again for the article.

"The flow of ice into the sea would probably raise sea levels about 10 feet rather than 20 feet, according to the analysis, published in the May 15 issue of the journal Science.

The scientists also predicted that seas would rise unevenly, with an additional 1.5-foot increase in levels along the east and west coasts of North America. That is because the shift in a huge mass of ice away from the South Pole would subtly change the strength of gravity locally and the rotation of the Earth, the authors said.

Several Antarctic specialists familiar with the new study had mixed reactions to the projections. But they and the study's lead author, Jonathan L. Bamber of the Bristol Glaciology Center in England, agreed that the odds of a disruptive rise in seas over the next century or so from the buildup of greenhouse gases remained serious enough to warrant the world's attention.

The study was carried out at Bristol University and soon other studies will follow as the years pass. In twenty years, however, we will all know the truth i.e. sea level did not rise. By then some study will deny the sea rise and start admitting that sea levels are falling.

The only danger here is that all the scientific media hype will force small Island states and low lying countries to spend a large part of their nation's budgets on unnecessary coastal defenses. In twenty years they will all realize that they were duped into expending large sums on a non event.

In Lompoc California the Johns Mansfield Company has a huge mining operation up on a mountain some miles from the sea. They mine diatomaceous material. Diatoms are microscopic alga: marine creatures that were deposited in the sea eons ago. Their sheer number formed the undersea mountain chain. The sea finally receded leaving the diatomaceous mountain... The tiny creatures are cellular in structure. Their cellular structure is used to make efficient industrial fuel filters

In keeping with what I have been advocating about receding seas. I think that some explanation is necessary to really grasp he essence. All our levels on land are taken from sea level. All municipalities around the world take their land levels from sea level, whatever sea levels happen to be in their location. Sea levels vary around the world so each locality takes their sea level as a datum. They average the difference between high and low tides and take the mean or average and so establish Mean Sea Level (MSL) for their particular municipality. Surveyors who have to take levels each and every day do not have to refer back to sea level each time they want to do a survey. The city performs this duty for them by providing what is known as benchmarks. Benchmarks are placed at convenient locations all over city streets. The benchmark is a usually a circular metal object imbedded flush with the sidewalk. They are placed at specific elevation above sea level. Most of us walk over them without knowing what they are. When a surveyor wants to carry out a survey on a particular street all he has to do is call the survey department of his city. They will fax him out a list of all the benchmarks in the particular area. All the surveyor has to do is find the most convenient benchmark that suits his survey. He then sets up his instrument over the benchmark and immediately knows his elevation above sea level. He then starts his survey. The Surveyor may be laying out a street or the floor level for a new house or a property boundary or any number of objectives. But the one thing he did not have to do is go back and start his survey at sea level. This is a good thing for the surveyor but it has a lot of drawbacks. These benchmarks have been the basis for much misaligned scientific theories. Over a period of fifty years, for example, these benchmarks are used continuously to establish levels. After fifty years when the city does a resurvey to establish new benchmark they find that the old benchmarks are terribly wrong. They first of all check sea level and start all over again. The old benchmarks, they find, are two feet higher than when they were established. The natural assumption is that the land has risen from the sea, they use the term rebounded.

They do not question sea level because sea level is always an accepted constant. So the theory of Isostatic Rebound was born to explain this anomaly. The theory states that the land is rebounding from the sea. The fact is that the sea is actually receding but we are conditioned to accept that the sea is a constant. It is because we insist on accepting sea level as a constant that we deny ourselves exciting scientific discoveries. As simple as it may seem acceptance of sea level decline will open up vast scientific possibilities. We will find solutions to many scientific problems that now confound us.

In the year 1013 construction started on the Abbey San Michel off the Normandy coast of France. The Abbey was built on a rock five miles out at sea in the English Channel. At that time there was a 45 foot tide that washed the rock as it went out and came in. That was in 1013. In the latter part of the nineteenth century the authorities built a causeway out to the Abbey. As the years passed it was noticed that the tide was moving further and further out away from the Normandy shoreline. In the last twenty years it became obvious that the sea would eventually desert the shoreline and even desert the Abbey and the rock it sat on. Today when you look out at the Abbey it is possible to walk out to it at low tide. The tide only surrounds the Abbey two times each month in recent times. In a few years the causeway will become unnecessary because it will be possible to walk to the Abbey. The sea had drawn away from the Shoreline of Normandy over the nearly one thousand year's sine the abbey started construction. The 45 foot tide has all but disappeared.

FIG. 1
THE MAJOR FAULTS OF NORTH AMERICA

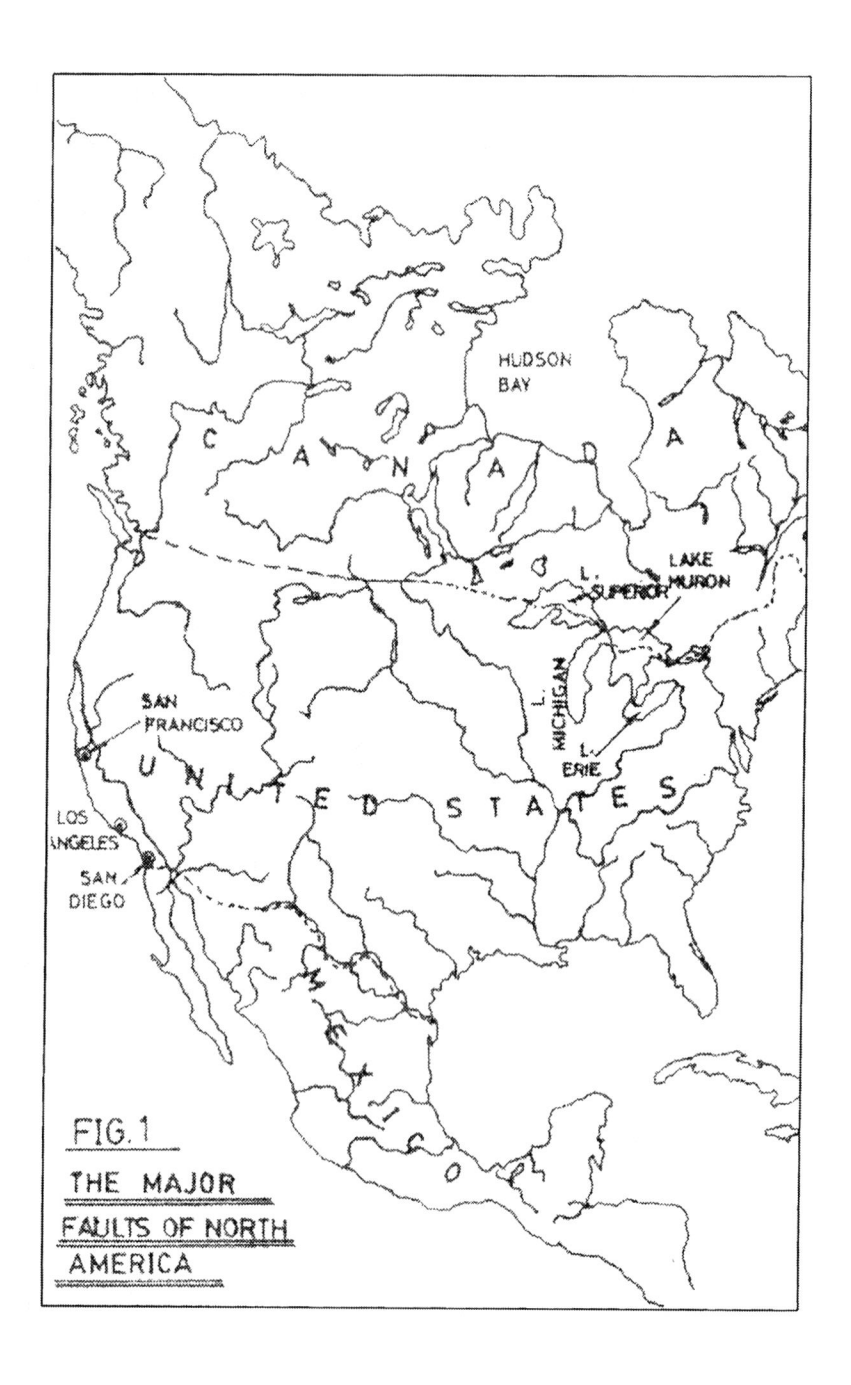

FIG. 2   WORLD OCEAN FLOOR : TECTONICS

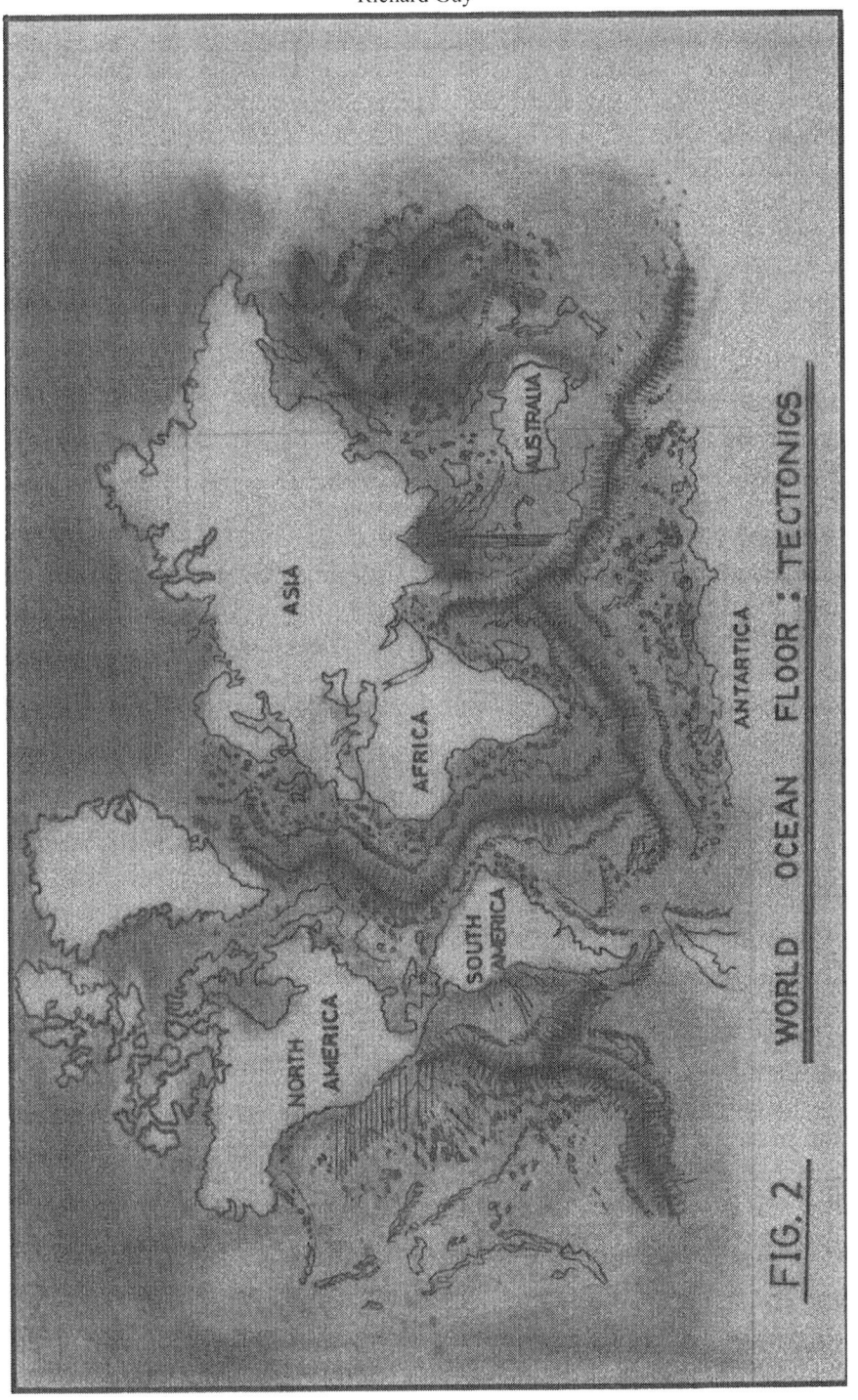

FIG. 3
THE SAN ANDREAS FAULT

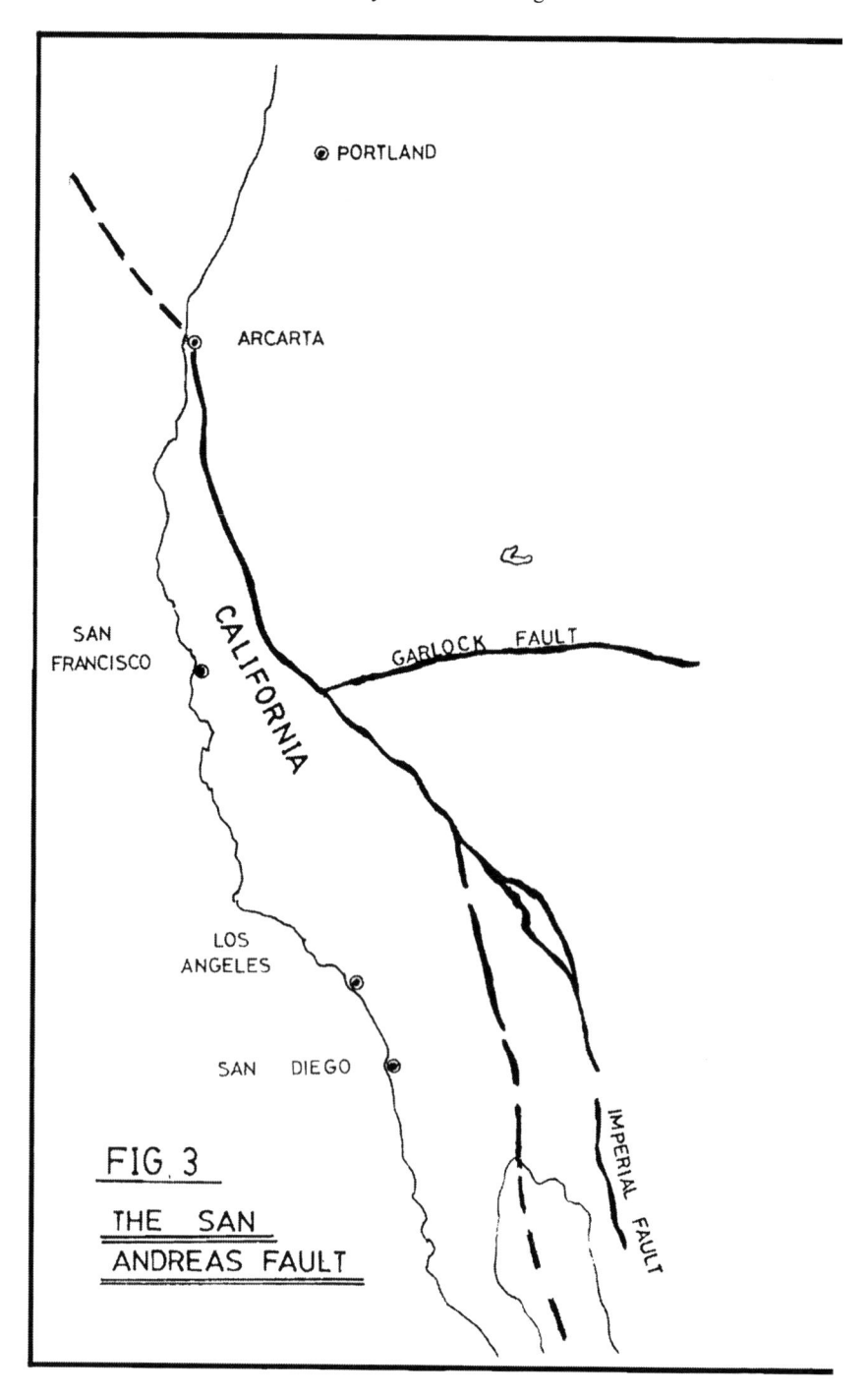

FIG. 4
SUMERIA

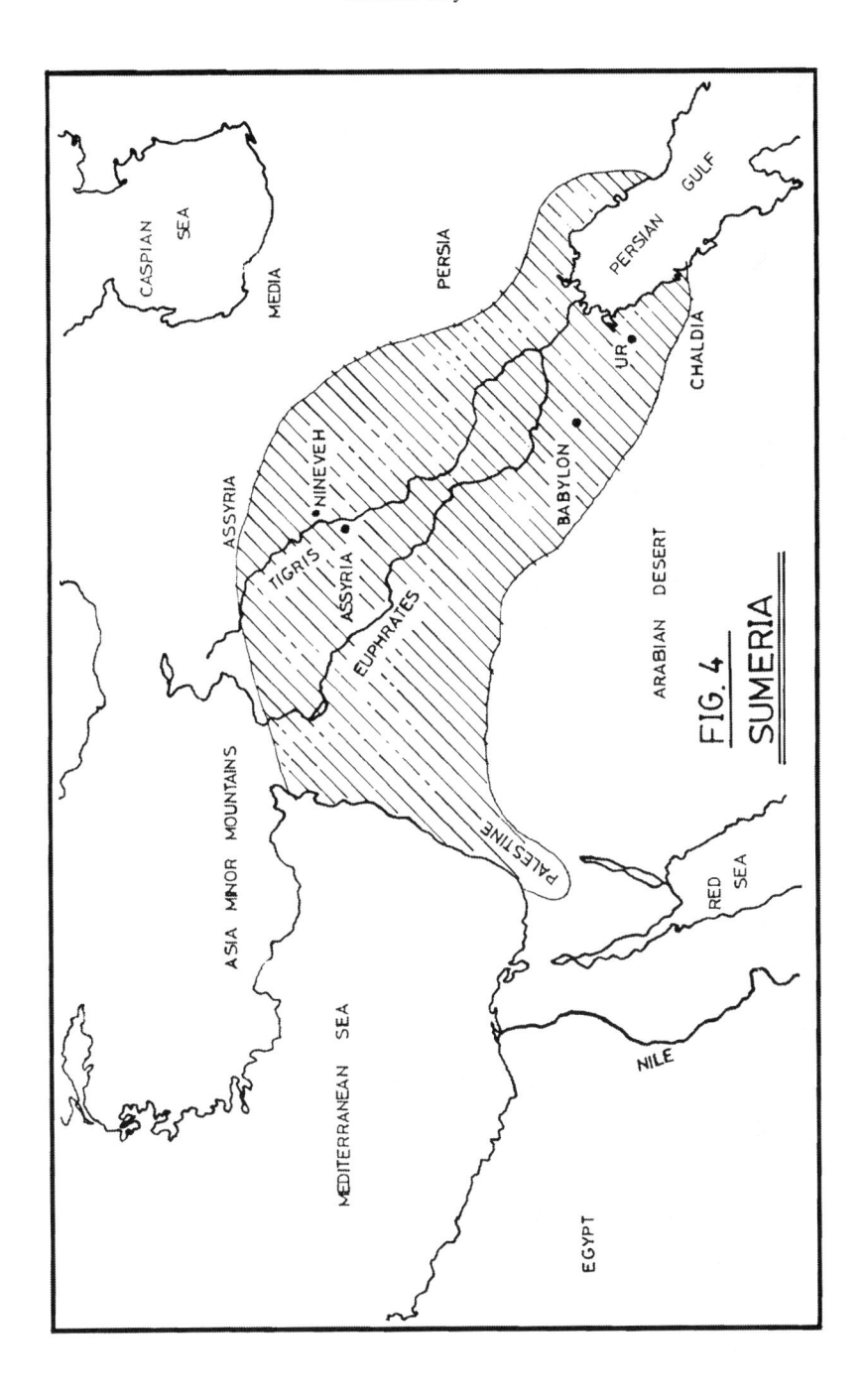

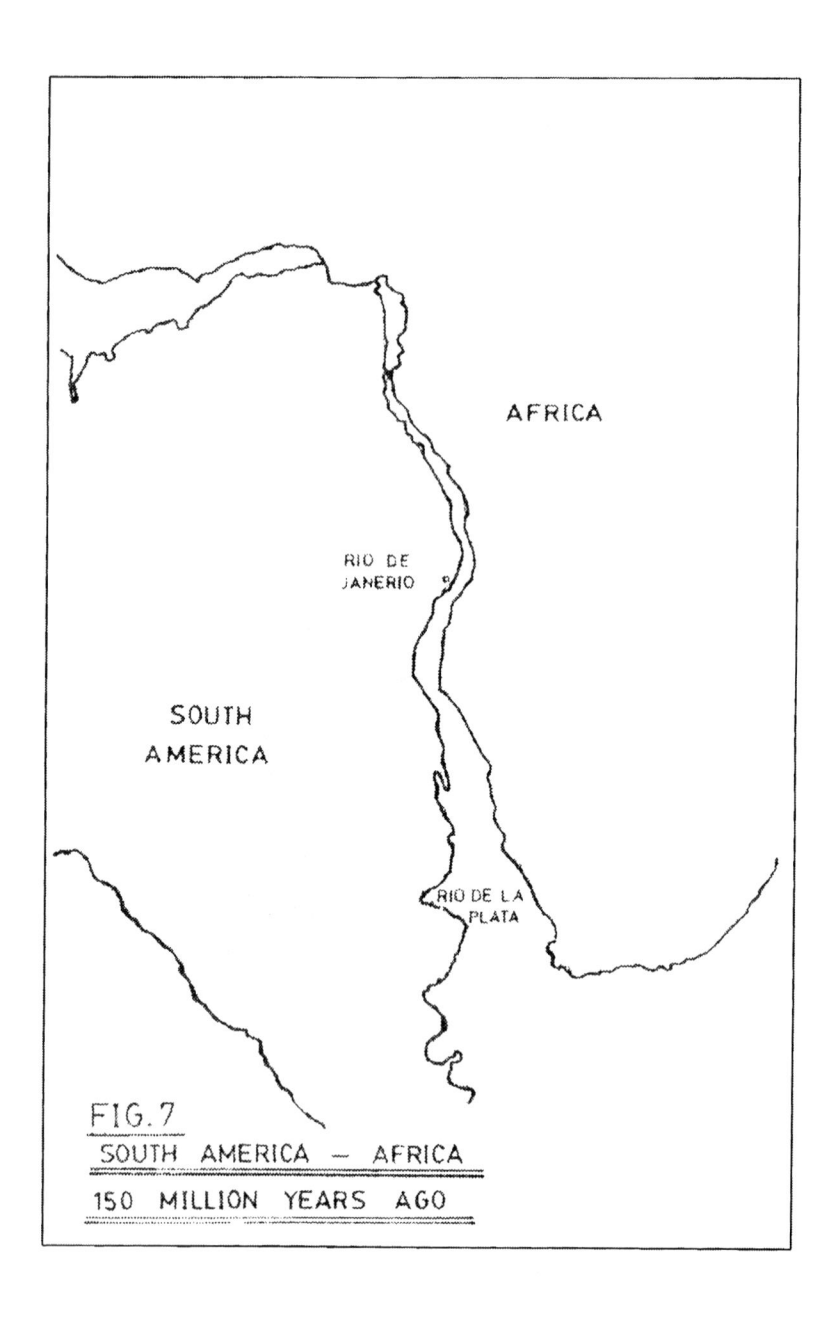

FIG. 7
SOUTH AMERICA — AFRICA
150 MILLION YEARS AGO

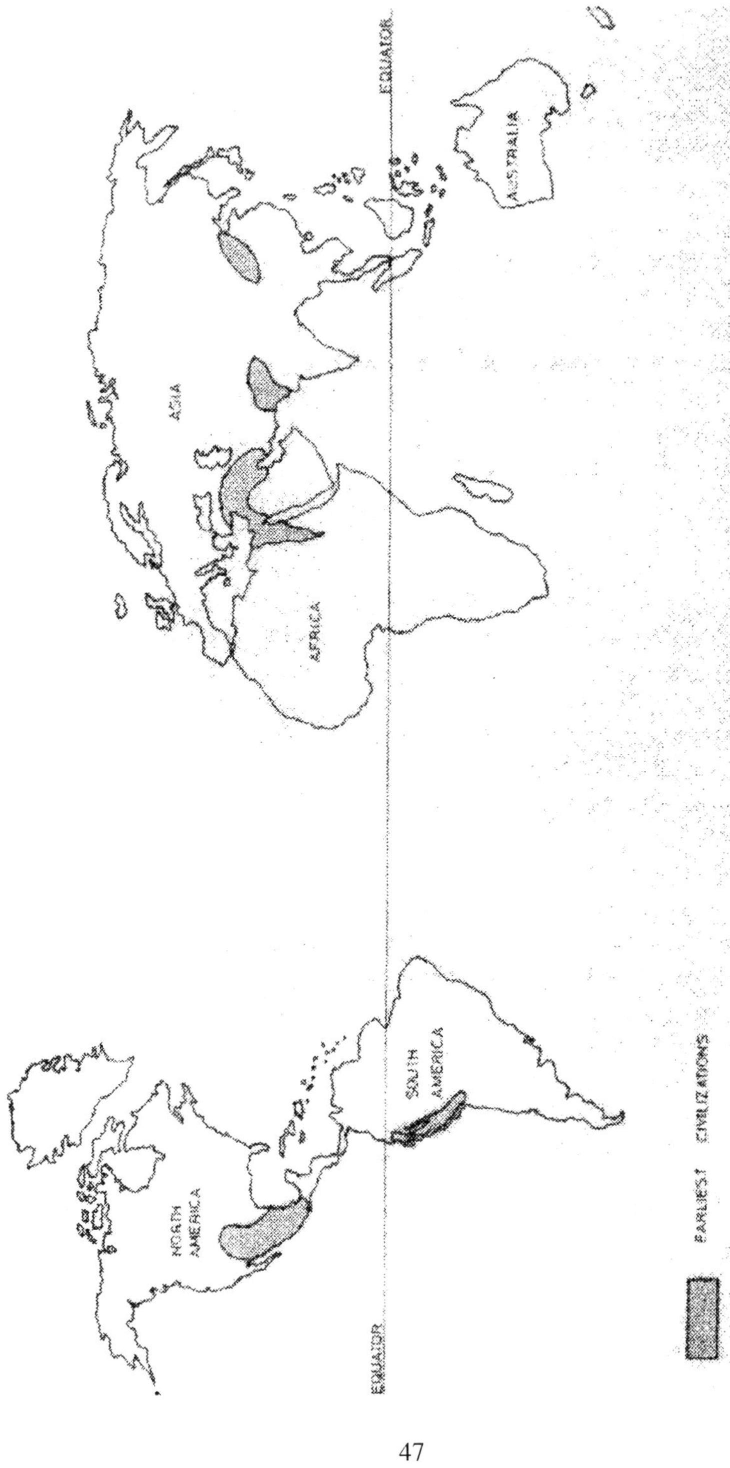

FIG. 8 — LOCATIONS OF THE EARLIEST CIVILIZATIONS

FIG. 9
THE HIGH PLAINS
HOME OF THE DINOSAURS

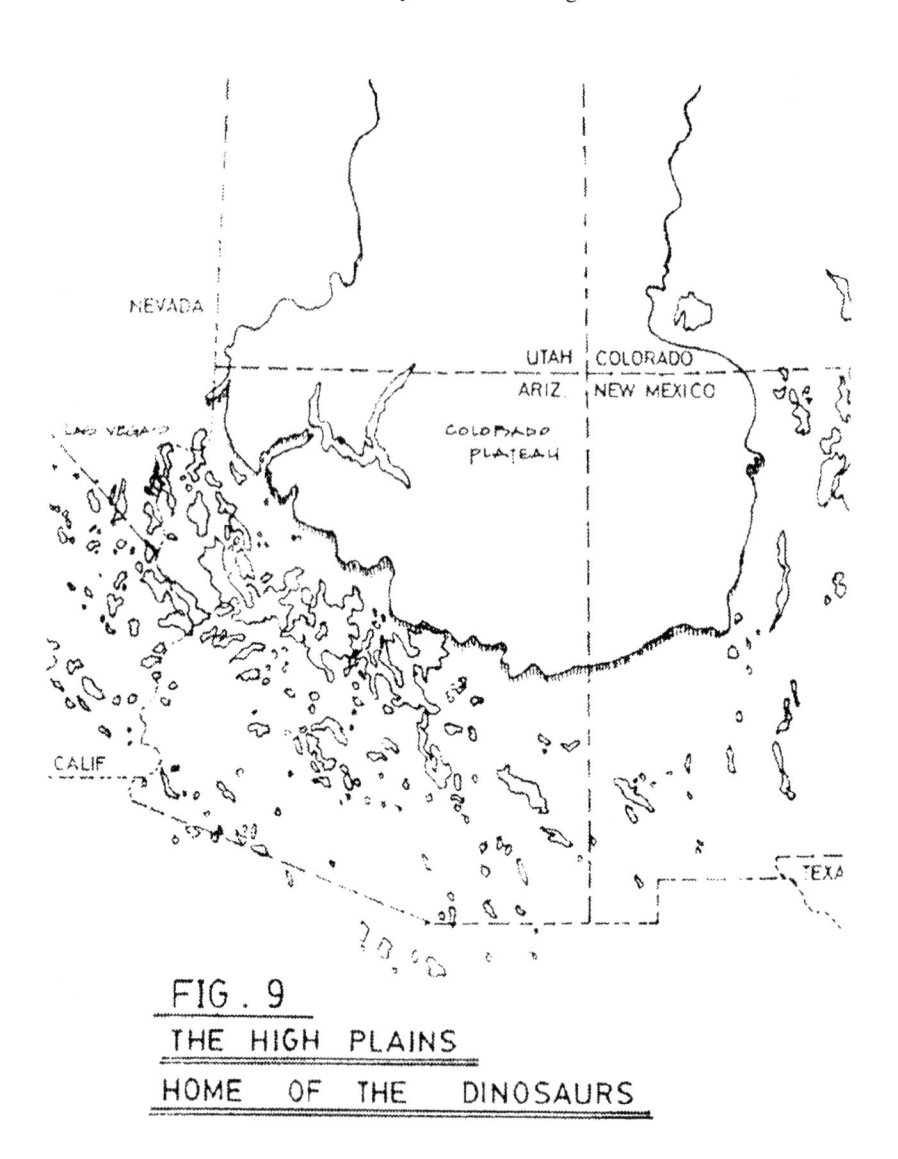

FIG. 10
INCA CIVILIZATION
&
INCA CITIES

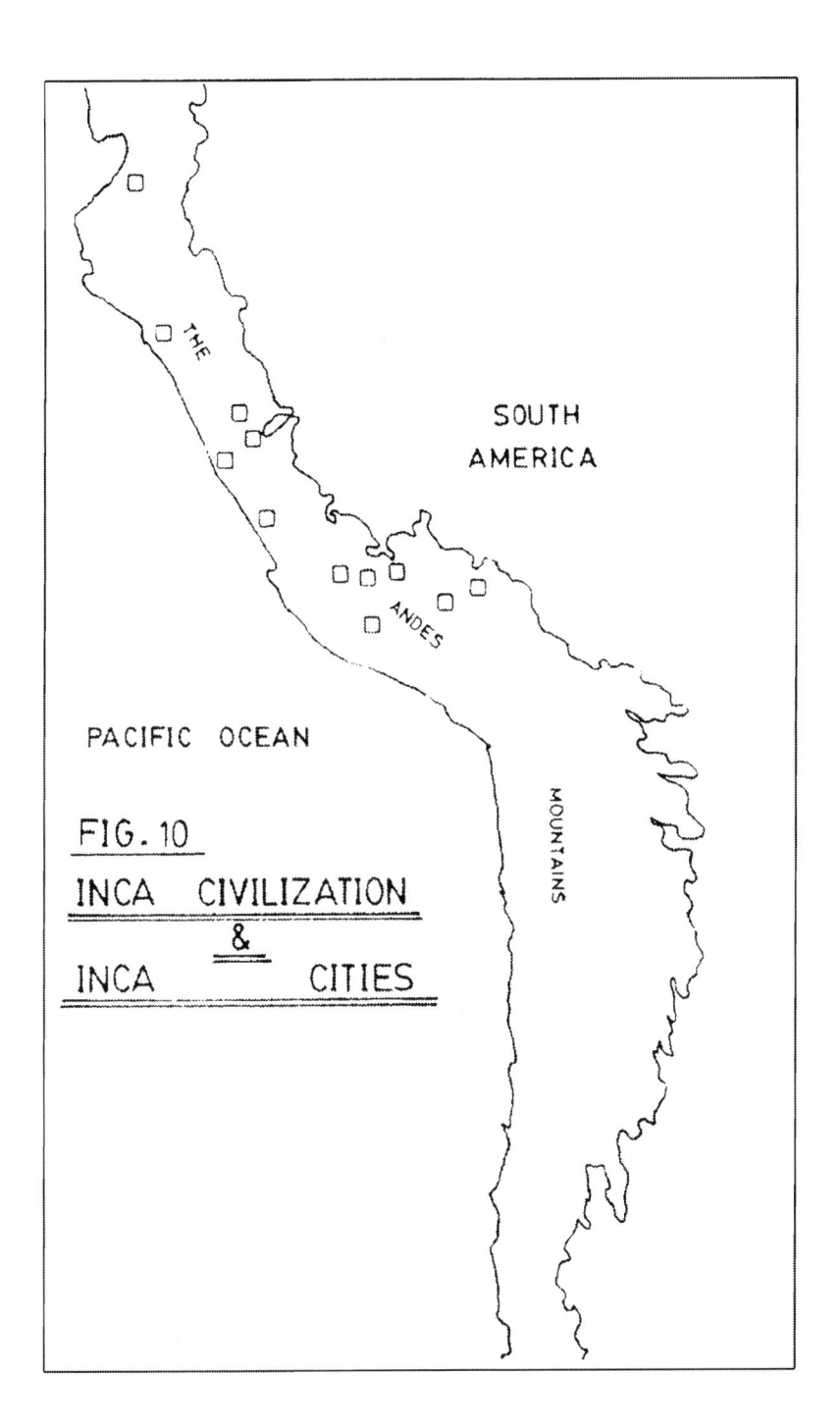

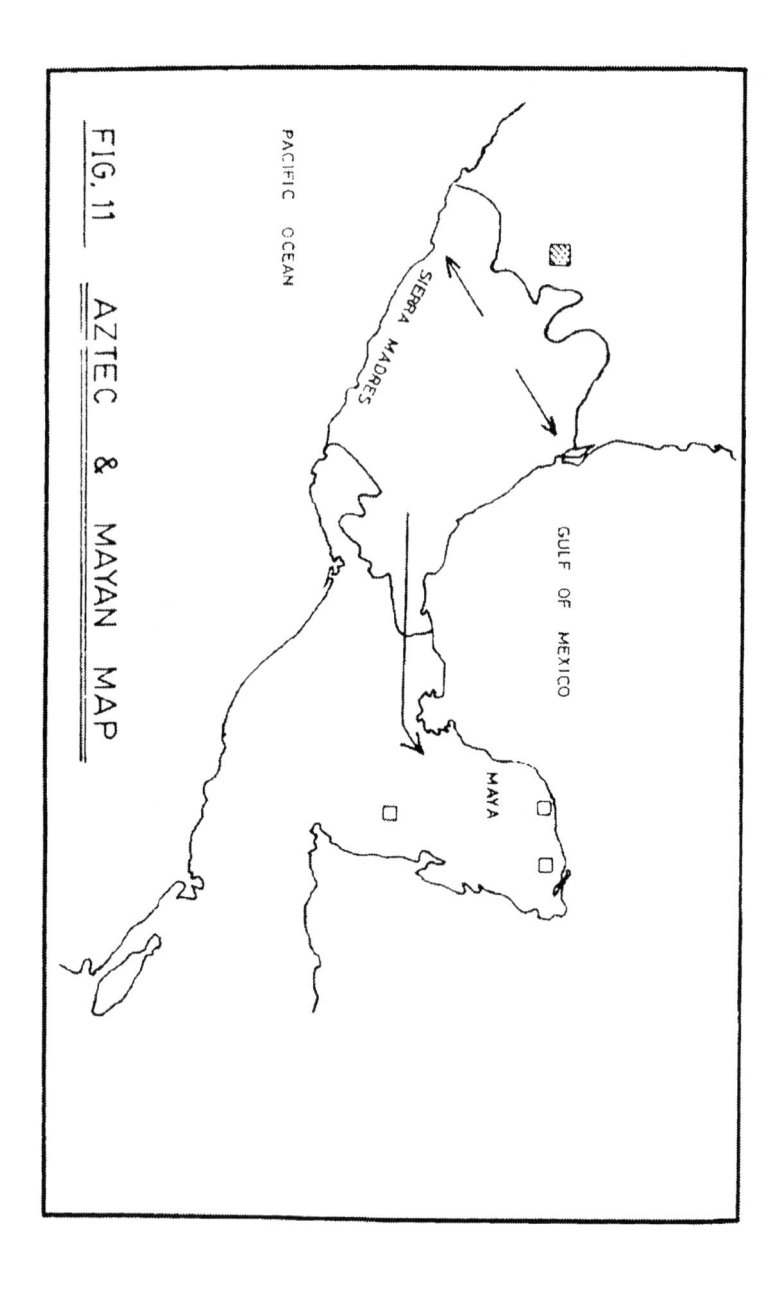

The Mysterious Receding Seas

FIG. 11 AZTEC & MAYAN MAP

FIG. 12   EGYPT

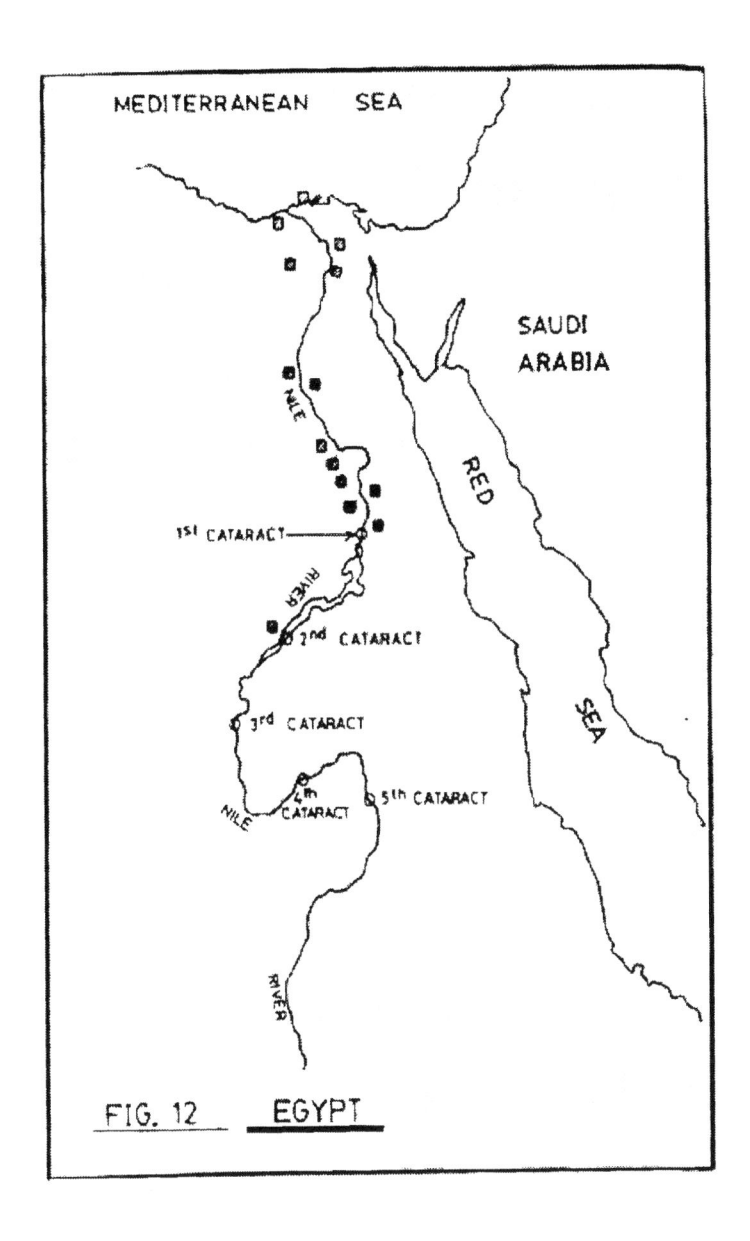

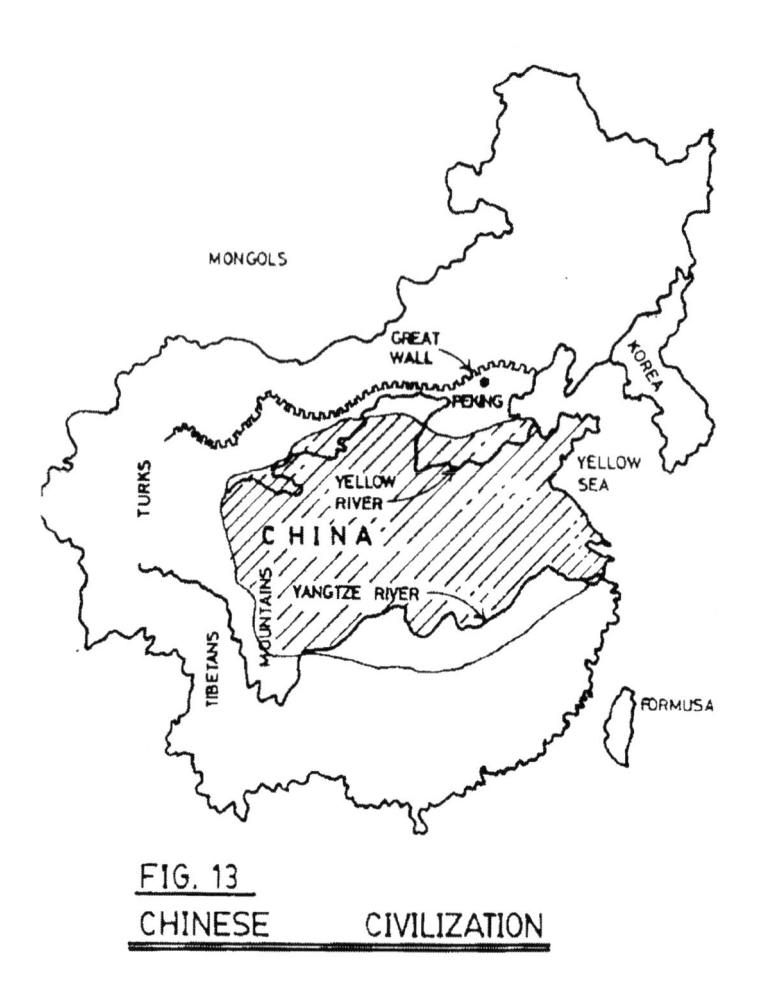

The Mysterious Receding Seas

FIG. 13
CHINESE CIVILIZATION

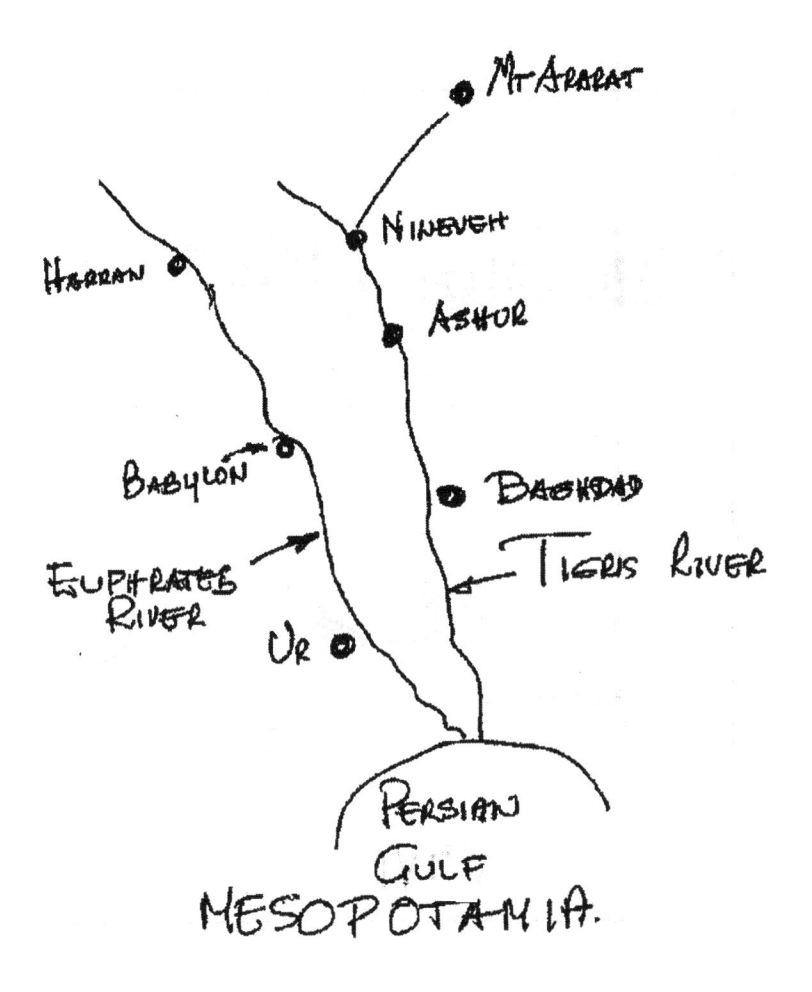

MESOPOTAMIA BETWEEN THE RIVERS.
Showing all the cities built after Nineveh, in a downward progression, as the sea receded.

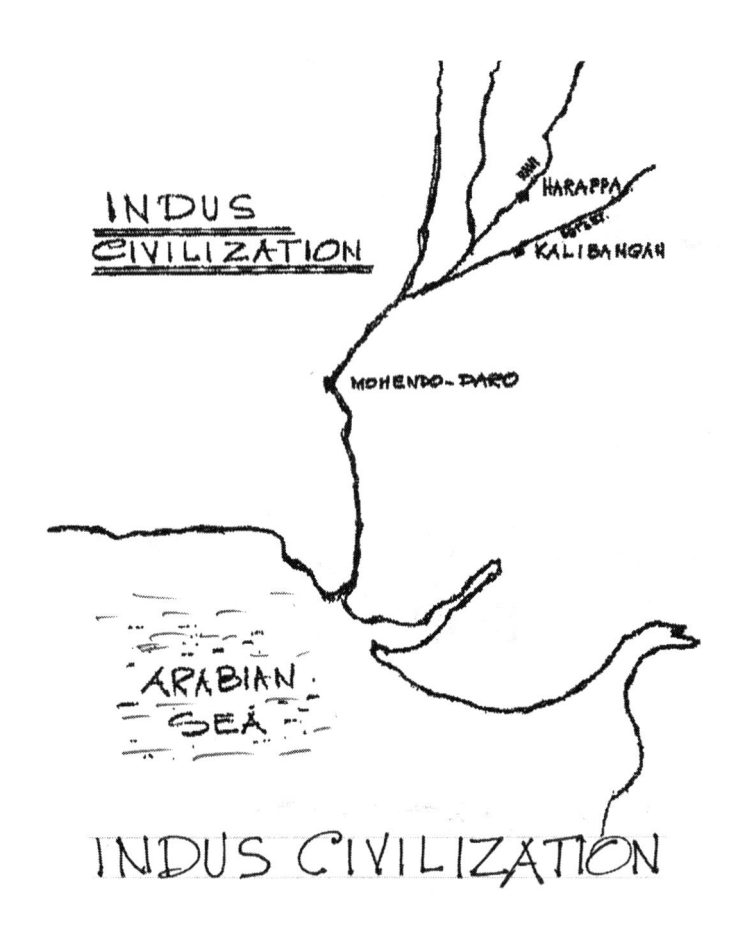

The Mysterious Receding Seas

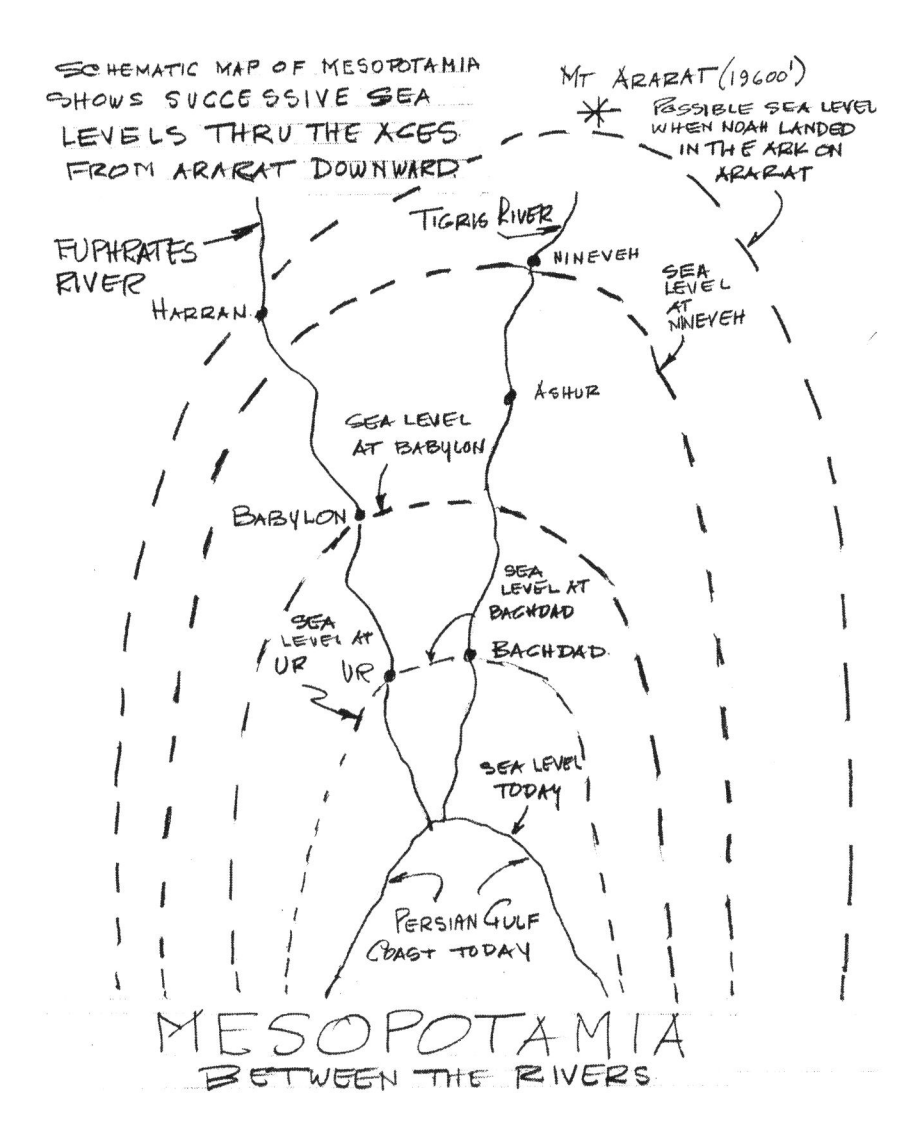

MESOPOTAMIA BETWEEN THE RIVERS.
Showing successive sea levels through the ages.

The Mysterious Receding Seas

Tjehenu

2nd millennium harbor works
Sebennytos
Sais • Tell-Nabasta
Komel-Hisn • Pi-Ramesse
Athribis • Tell el-Daba
Tell el-Yahudiya

Giza ▲ Heliopolis
Saqqara ■ •
Memphis •
El-Lisht • Dahshur
Hawara Sarabit el-K
Medinet Ma'adi ▲ El-Lahun Wadi Maghara
Kom Medinet Ghurab

Bahariya oasis

Heracleopolis

Beni Hasan •
El-Ashmunein ▲▲• El-Sheikh Ibada
Farafra oasis El-Amarna • Deir el-Bersha Gebel el-Zeit
Meir □ Hatnub

Western Desert

Asyut • □
Qaw el-Kebir Mersa Gawasis

ANCIENT CAPITAL

Akhmim
• Abydos
Thebes ▲ Valley of the Kings
Armant

Dakhla oasis

El-Kab
Hieraconpolis •
Bala ▲ Edfu Wadi Beiza

ANCIENT EGYPT

El-Kharga oasis
Gebel el-Silsila Wadi Khat
Aswan
Elephantine Wadi el-H

Tjemeh

Dunqul oasis

LAKE NASSAR

Amada Beit el-Wali
Gerf Husein
El-Sebua
Abu Simbel Aniba El-Derr
Abahuda
Buhen

Wawat

Faras
Semna Uronarti
Aksha
Kumma
Amara
Sedeinga
Sdeb
Sesebi

THE NEW KINGDOM

Symbol	Meaning
□	Nubian gold resources
—	Trade routes
▲	Temple
▭	Royal tomb
□	Major provincial tomb
▰	Mines and quarries
▬	Fortifications
▬	Court cemetery
□	Copper and tin sources

Cush

Kawa
Napata
Gebel Barkal

I R E M

56

Photo of Mount San Michel on the coast of Normandy surrounded by sea.

The Mysterious Receding Seas

Mount San Michele as it looks today surrounded by mud flats and deserted by the sea. The causeway was built 100 years ago. The Abbey was built on a Rock 5 Kilometers out at sea in 1013 but today the sea has deserted it: It will soon be part of the mainland. The tidal fluctuation around the Abbey was 45 feet but it has now ebbed leaving the Abbey high and dry in 1000 years

Castle St Michel Mount at Penzance off the coast of Cornwall, UK. You can now walk to the castle from the coast.

Author standing astride the Eastern and Western Hemispheres at the Meridian at Greenwich, England The Meridian has moved 60 feet over from where the author is standing

This Earthquake fault in Lampoc California destroyed an old Spanish Monastery in its path in 1811-1812 :the same earthquake that destroyed New Madrid, Kansas

The Afar fault Which is splitting Africa; the Red Sea will eventually flow into the fault.

The Tibet Fault: Tibetans gather salt from the deposits left behind by ancient seas at 18000 feet above today's sea level.

The Mysterious Receding Seas

CHAPTER 3

In the eighteenth century the Barbary Coast Pirates terrorized the North African Coast. The spread terror all around the Mediterranean and after awhile ventured out into the Atlantic in search of ships to plunder. They were merciless and captured men women and children. They took their captives back to North Africa to a life of slavery and abuse. In time their exploits reached England and Ireland.

The quiet Cornish town of Penzance is located in the south of England. One Sunday morning while the seaside church was holding service the Pirates raided and emptied the church. Three hundred unsuspecting worshipers were herded down to their ships and taken away to North Africa to a life of slavery. The Gilbert and Sullivan Operetta, "The Pirates of Penance" is a parody on this atrocious event that occurred over two hundred years ago.

When I visited Penzance I wanted to see the church where the infamous act took place so many years ago. I had stopped beside a little seaside church thinking that that might be the one but I was wrong. I asked around to see if anyone knew the story of the pirates and I asked about the church. A young lady kindly volunteered to show me the pirate church. She led my wife and me over a little hillock to higher ground and then behind the hill she showed me the old church. She pointed out that the little church by the seaside was built in recent times in relation to the sea. The church she further allowed is about the same distance from the sea as the old church was two hundred years ago before the sea receded. She continued to point our many features of interest. She pointed out the municipal swimming pool built on the sea front. "The swimming pool was built on land that was once under the sea" she said.

One of the attractions of Penzance is the castle that sits on a rock two miles offshore. The Castle is St Micheal Mount. The Castles is related to Mount San Michal off the Normandy Coast of France. In 1067, the monastery of Mount-Saint Michel gave its support to duke William of Normandy in his claim to the throne of England. It was rewarded with properties and grounds on the English side of the Channel, including a small island located at the West of Corwall. Saint Michael,s Mount was built on the little Island.

It became a Norman Priory and is located off the coast of Cornwall in the town of Penzance.

Years ago the Castle was surrounded by a huge tidal fluctuation. A causeway was built to gain access to the Castle at high tide. Today however it is possible to walk to the Castle Rock as the tide has departed.

The Town of Sandwich is on the South Eastern coastline of Britain. In the Middle Ages Sandwich boasted the largest harbor in Britain. It boasted that its harbor could accommodate the entire British Navy, Well we also have to consider that the ships were much smaller then. At any rate the harbor was large enough to boast about. The Town of Sandwich is on the River Stour. Over the years the river silted up and Sandwich lost it harbor. Today the town is two miles inland deserted by the receding sea.

Sandwich is the birth place of the earl of Sandwich from who the famous Sandwich gets it name. It is also the birth place of Thomas Paine one of the fathers of the American Revolution and Sydney Greenstreet the famous movie actor. It is also one of the Cinque Ports along the southeast of Britain. There are five Cinque Ports. Sandwich, Dover, Hythe Romney and Hastings.

The Cinque Ports were called upon to supply boats to ferry troops across the channel in times of war. The king gave the towns special concessions such as tax free status for the favor. This had been the policy since the middle ages.

During the WW2 however they again served king and country in the evacuation from Dunkirk.

In 1940 British troops were retreating from France after the Germans captured Dunkirk. There were 400000 British troops to be evacuated and there was a shortage of naval vessels in place to do the job. The troops were under heavy bombardment by the Germans and the troops had to be evacuated under heavy fire.

Then, as if out of nowhere, fishing boats, pleasure yachts, and even lifeboats arrived by the hundreds, seeking to rescue the British and French troops seeking exile from Nazi-dominated Europe. Braving mines, bombs, and torpedoes, civilians of all stripes manned their boats and came to the rescue. German planes had bombed the harbor, so the soldiers had to be ferried from the beaches to the waiting boats.

Once again the Cinque Ports had risen to the occasion. Churchill referred to them as his Armada.

Great storms of 1787 silted up the river and blocked off the river with sandbanks and the isolation of Sandwich began. Today the Town is two miles inland. All the land rolling down to the sea has been converted into golf courses and the British open was held there in 1983. If you ask the townspeople today how the town came to be so far from the sea they would say that the river silted up. They pay no attention to the fact that there is a gradient going down to the sea which indicated that the sea level had dropped through the ages. Of course we see this decline in sea levels all along the British coast.

The Town of Richborough is close to Sandwich and during the Roman occupation of Britain Richborough was a Roman Naval Base and had its own harbor. Today however Richborough is also two miles inland cut off completely from the sea.

It is interesting to note also that over the years since the Middle Ages all the ports along the coast have lost their harbors.

Today only Dover has a harbor and that is because they have rebuilt their harbor many times as the sea shallowed. They also did not have a river to deposit silt on their foreshore.

Today Hastings, Romney, Hythe and Sandwich are all isolated from the sea.

All the old Roman Roads in Britain were built on the sea in Roman Times but today they are all inland which shows clearly where the sea was at that time.

Christopher Columbus was born in Genoa his house is still there overlooking the Mediterranean. There is a sea wall in front of his house which bears no relationship to the sea level today. Housing goes right down to the sea where there is another breakwater

Columbus no doubt had very good seagoing experience for he sailed for many years as the captain for the Centurione Bankers in Rome. The maps that Columbus sailed with were made by a clever Jewish Cartographer by the name of Cresque. Columbus was fascinated with the seas recession as he noted it along the coast in front of his house.

Another interesting aside was that Columbus had a lot of prior knowledge of discovery before he sailed. The Roman Catholic Church had established missions in Greenland four hundred years before Columbus sailed on his voyage of discovery. Reports kept coming back to Rome of the savages that attacked the mission to steal the cattle. Columbus must have known of such inhabitants through his connections.

Years later when he was in the Azores on the most westerly Island in the Island chain. He heard a commotion down on the beach where a crowd had gathered. When he went to investigate he saw a small canoe with three dead Indians in it. In Columbus own words. "I could see from the color of their skin that they were not Christian. They wore clothes of an intricate weave not known to us in Europe;" Columbus figured that if the Indians could come across the sea without sails he could reach them with sails. Of course it was obvious that the unfortunate Indians had been carried along by the Gulf Stream from the shores of the Americas.

So when Columbus sailed he had good prior intelligence of the possibilities ahead.

It is also very pointed that the timing of his sailing coincided with the enactment of the Inquisition order in Spain. All Jews were to leave Spain by July 31st 1492. Columbus sailed on August 3rd 1492 Three days after the order came into effect. This momentous departure speaks volumes for the timing and the temperature of that pivotal time in the history of the Eastern and the Western Hemispheres. At that time it was reported that 300000 Jews were on the docks in Spain awaiting any ship that would take them away from Spain. Columbus sailed from Spain on a sea that was perhaps ten feet higher than sea level today.

The port of Genoa, where Columbus was born, is near to Pisa on the Italian Coast. Early Records of the Construction of the famous tower relate it proximity to the sea. Today however it is far from the sea.

Today the A12 autostrada passes through Pisa. The A12 is approximately one mile from the Tower. Back in historical times the sea was half mile further back that the autostrada towards the tower. So the A12 autostrada is built on lands that were once under the Mediterranean Sea.

The same anomaly is noted all around the Mediterranean from Gibraltar to Syria and from Egypt to Morocco. The sea has retreated significantly from all ports around the coastline. Any harbor authority in 1737 would not have known of the receding sea. Today after almost three hundred years the situation remains the same. They all say their harbors have sited up so they have to build new ones. Palos and Barcelona have had to make major shoreline adjustments since 1737 to keep their ports open. The estuary of the Rhone River in France comes out in the Bay of Lions. The river delta has moved out twelve miles in the years since 1737. The harbor of Marseilles further along the French coast has had to build an entirely new harbor because of, they say, the siltation problem. They blame the siltation problem on the Rhone River deposits. They have also built another harbor at the turn of the century. That one was demolished by the Germans when they retreated in World War 2. A new harbor has been built since. The Harbor at Genoa, Italy has been rebuilt and extended during the last two hundred years for the same reason: the receding seas.

The most conclusive proof that seas once covered all of the earth is that salt deposits are to be found on every continent on earth. Ancient seas left these deposits all over the world. The Sahara Desert sits on a large deposit of salt and so do the Gobi desert and every other desert on earth. There are mountains of salt in Russia and there are underground salt deposits in Europe and the United States. All these deposits were left there by ancient seas. In the mountains of San Lazario near El Paso in Texas you can drive through salt dunes left there thousands of years ago. In California Borax is mined from deposits left there by ancient seas. In China salt deposits are everywhere. In Tibet the inhabitants mine salt from the bed of an ancient sea which no longer exists. Strange as it may sound the ancient sea bed is at eighteen thousand feet above sea level. You have to ask where the sea has gone from that height to the level it is today. Your answer must be that the seas are receding... You cannot wonder where the sea has gone unless you ask how did sea level fall to where it s today? The answer must be the expansion of the earth.

Another indication of ancient seas is the skeletal remains of whales and dinosaurs all over the world. The remains of Whales are to be found on every continent on earth. All across Canada and the United States remains of whales have been found. The Island of Montreal sits in the St Lawrence River. Whale remains have been found in Montreal. Montreal is seven hundred feet above sea level. The Bible story tells us that Jonah was swallowed by a large fish and deposited in Nineveh. Nineveh is seven hundred feet above sea level. It is quite likely that Nineveh was once on the shores of the Persian Gulf. We know that Babylon was once on the coast and so was Ur and Baghdad. So why not Nineveh in the progression of the seas recession.

In 1980 when The Expanding Earth Exchange was inaugurated. All known theory adherents were asked to contribute articles for the first publication. I am proud that my article was included in the first and subsequent editions. The complete list of these contributors can be seen in the archives of the Expanding Earth Exchange; www.expanding-earth.org. All the contributors came from various professional disciplines. What impressed me most of all was that all the contributors had come to the realization that our planet was expanding and all had arrived at their conclusion from observations made in their own particular profession. There is a large diversity of opinions all expressing the same theory; but all arriving at their conclusions from different viewpoints.

The debate about Earth Expansion will no doubt go on for a long time. It is my hope that new thinking will be introduced. As I mentioned previously the earth has two faces, it shows us one but hides the other. We make assumptions at face value such as sea level. Sea level is an illusion like many the other assumptions we have made for the last two hundred years. We have to unmask the earth and strip her of her pretenses. e.g.

Sea level does not rise: the seas recede. Mountains don't grow; it is the sea level that falls. All other anomalies we observe within these basic parameters have legitimate explanations. Stated another way it amounts to this. Many of the theories of the past have been based on assumptions that were wrong. The earth deceived the observer. Because of this we have to strike out for ourselves and seek the truth by unmasking the earth. We want to see her real face. We know that the earth is deceptive. We can no longer afford to be deceived.

My major concern is that small Island states and low lying countries will be misled into spending a large portion of their budgets on coastal defenses. The constant media hype and bias towards rising sea levels is forcing this issue upon small nations. International lending agencies are behind the hype to sell the threat of rising seas. They are lined up to make loans which future generations, yet unborn, will have to repay. Small nations are being lead into this trap which is a catch 22 trap for them. These governments cannot defy the popular hype: fold their arms and do nothing. Their constituents naturally want them, as their leaders, to act in their protection. So they have to borrow and build coastal defenses. These coastal defenses will in a few short years prove to be unnecessary because the seas are receding not rising. A study coming out of Bristol University is halving the forecasted twenty foot rise in sea levels over the next century. What they are saying is that sea levels will not rise as much as forecasted. They say it will be nearer ten feet over that period. These studies all treat sea level as a datum that never changes. There lies the weakness in the hypothesis. The assumptions on which sea level rise are made is that sea level is constant. What we, therefore, have to do is to introduce receding seas into the equation... There will actually be no sea level rise in one hundred years.

All the money spent on coastal defenses will have been for a non event.

Events related in the Bible are another indicator of the height of sea levels back in biblical times. The Biblical story of Noah is an important analogy. When Noah's Ark came to rest on the top of Mount Ararat he had been Bourne on the flood for forty days and forty nights. He disembarked with his wife and three sons on to dry land. God gave him explicit instructions "Go forth and multiply and replenish the earth' God has erased all humankind with the flood because he was displeased with them. Noah and his family wandered off to start their lives anew. Noah lived on after to flood another one hundred and fifty years the bible tells us. After his death the sons and their children wandered on. Now if the Ark landed on Mount Ararat, the top of a mountain there is nowhere else to go but downward. So eventually Noah's grandson Nimrod established the city of Nineveh on the Tigris River. When we look at the Map of Iraq we see that the Location of Nineveh is directly related to the downward path that the progeny of Noah would have taken. It was a natural location on a downward trend. The City of Nineveh was the Capital of the Assyrian Nation. Noah is hailed as the Patriarch of the Assyrian

Nation. The Bible sets out the progeny of Noah in great detail. It also says that Noah's Progeny went out in all

Directions to populate the earth. What is interesting here is that historians tell us that Nineveh was the oldest city in Assyria and we can well believe it. What historians omit to tell us, only because they don't really know, is that not only is Nineveh the oldest city in Assyria but it is the first city built in Mesopotamia. All other cities in Mesopotamia coming down the Tigris and Euphrates Rivers were built after Nineveh in descending order of age. That is to say that all the other cities were built after Nineveh in downward progression. Nineveh was indeed the oldest and also the first.

Today Nineveh is seven hundred feet above sea level but in ancient times it was on the Persian Gulf. How do we know this? Ur of the Chaldees was the Birthplace of Abraham the Patriarch of the Jewish Nation. When Abraham was born in Ur it was a busy seaport on the Persian Gulf. Today However. Ur is two hundred miles from the gulf and one hundred and thirty five feet above sea level.

In ancient times Baghdad, also, was a harbor on the Persian Gulf but today Baghdad is three hundred and fifty miles from the Gulf and One hundred and twenty five feet above sea level. Today Nineveh is one thousand miles from the sea.

Jonah the Prophet lived in Nineveh and ran away to sea and was swallowed by a Whale. Jonah did not run away one thousand miles to be swallowed by a whale. He ran away to a sea that was quite close to Nineveh.

Ancient legends tell us that ancient monsters came from the sea to teach the Babylonians science and mathematics as well as building and Architecture. Each night the monsters, half man and half fish returned to the sea. Each day they came from the sea to keep on teaching the Babylonians to advance their civilizations. They returned to the sea each night. The sea must have been close to Babylon in those days for certainly the monsters did not travel four hundred miles to the sea each night. The ruins of the ancient city of Babylon are four hundred miles from the sea today.

The greatest Misconception is Sea Level Datum; there is no such thing. Sea level is an illusion: we don't know sea level. When we are told that sea levels are raising we do a great disservice to scientific advancement. This insistence on rising sea levels clouds the main issue and leads us further away from the truth. We have to look beyond this fallacy. We have to realize once and for all that sea levels are falling and will continue to fall as the earth expands. Environmental awareness has been heightened in the last fifty years. We look at all aspects of our atmosphere around us: we walk around with our heads in the clouds never bothering to look down. We continue to overlook the basis of our very existence: the earth and sea. About them: we know nothing. We cannot go on that way. We have to start looking at the seas and trying to analyze what is happening;

we have to find the missing link between the expansion process and our receding seas. When we do we will solve a plethora of other problems that now haunt our scientists. So much is being learned in all other fields that it is time to spend some time looking at our earth.

Does it not seem strange that the United States withdrew from signing the Kyoto Protocol? Why the sudden about turn to abstain from signing? In the arena of international affairs that does appear odd? What made the United States turn its back on this particular United Nations treaty? You can rest assured that there are motives over and beyond the actual reasons stated. All other U.N. member nations of the world, except four, have ratified the treaty. What secret or secrets does the United States hold? What secret is the United States holding back from the rest of the world? The United States has stated its reason? Is that the real reason? Wouldn't you like to know? First of all, the Kyoto Protocol is concerned with environmental issues. Greenhouse emissions and Global Warming are the moot points. Because of Global Warming the forecast is that sea levels will rise in ensuing years to swamp Low Countries worldwide. Smaller nations and especially island nations scrambled over each other in a panic to sign the treaty. They fear that in a few years their tiny island states would be inundated. Just how much of this is actually based on fact. How much of this generated fear is contrived. Let us look at what has been happening. Information easily available on the internet tells us that Global

Warming is a fact of life but not necessarily a function of greenhouse gasses or carbon emissions. The available information states quite clearly that if all the carbon emissions ceased immediately the earth will still continue to get hotter. The earth is generating its own internal heat. The United States knows this and that is not all it knows. It is for this, and a lot of other reasons that makes the U.S. refuse to sign. So, what does the United States know? Let us probe further. The United States has lead the world in GPS technology. Every point on the globe is crisscrossed by satellites, which pinpoint coordinates with great accuracy. The horizontal and vertical coordinates can be measured in millimeters of accuracy. This is a fantastic achievement considering that satellites hundreds of miles out in space make these measurements. The GPS surveillance of earth has made the compass literally useless. What has America learned from GPS surveys that they are not telling the world? Is GPS really as accurate as it is reputed to be? Let's see! When the United States first started sending satellites up to establish GPS certain anomalies on the earths surface became apparent. Over the long period of development of the technology it was discovered that coordinates moved around on the earth, they did not remain fixed. This discovery was made in the early days. At first, it was interpreted that the horizontal movement of the continental plates were responsible for the shifting coordinates. This, however, turned out to be only a part of the mystery. More fascinating findings were to come. There was no pattern to the movement but they moved. Following up on these discoveries, further anomalies were observed. Not only did coordinates move horizontally but also they moved vertically. Vertical coordinates, measured successively over time, were observed to be moving upward. Could the earth's surface be rising? This development puzzled the technicians, they had to make sure. This mysterious series of observations held earth-shattering implications for what was to come. The data collected over successive years posed a scientific enigma. As the vertical coordinates rose in elevation on the earth's surface the vertical coordinates of sea level fell. This mystery demanded re-examination of a plethora of data. Previously collected data was, again, scrutinized and analyzed. The findings were classified for two reasons. The first reason was that more time was needed to study the significance of the findings. The other was that if the data were correct Global Warming would be irrelevant. It was discovered that sea level datum was not fixed as we had been made to believe. As long as could be remembered, sea level datum was assumed to be a fixed reference point. All topographical elevations on earth are taken from Mean Sea Level Datum. That datum was never supposed to move. Now GPS had shown clearly that Mean Sea Level Datum was a myth. GPS revealed that sea level was falling constantly. Not only was it falling but also from all indications, had been doing so for a very long time. What were now emerging from the data were clear images of successive ancient shorelines. These shoreline images showed in wavelike fashion how far inland seas had reached in bygone eras. They were amazed at the extent of the seas encroachment. Not only did the sea encroach inland in ages past, old shorelines showed the heights reached by ancient seas covered all the continents. This new information brought with it a million questions. The major question to be answered was if, as had been clearly indicated, the seas were much higher and were still falling in level, what was the engine of displacement? Where was all that water that once covered the major part of the earth? Where had it all gone? Why was sea level creeping mysteriously lower and lower? It had always been assumed to be a fixed datum. So, why have we never heard anything about all these amazing discoveries? Why no announcements of these colossal findings? The reason is simple. As more and more data came in and was analyzed more earth shattering revelations came. All that we believed we knew or for that matter perceived we knew was being disproved by GPS. The constant change in the vertical coordinates of land and sea elevations meant only one thing. It could not be denied, the data did not lie. It was obvious that the earth was expanding. The conclusion was that the fall and retreat of seas from shorelines worldwide was a direct result of that expansion. The vertical rise of the earth coordinates indicated expansion. The vertical fall of sea levels indicated the outfall of the expansion process. Now, how were they to announce that planet earth was expanding? They definitely could not. Not at that moment, not at that time. The multiple discoveries were stupendous. All of a sudden, they were assailed by all this new information, which conflicted with all that had been known, and/or taught before. In one way, scientists had painted themselves into a corner. In another way, the information they now possessed had tremendous implications for all sciences. Serious consideration had to be given to the information overload.

CHAPTER 4

GPS was stirring up a hornet's nest of information contrary to what was, up to then, accepted thought. It showed that the earth was expanding. It was for years mainstream thought had propounded that the earth was constant in size. All theories about the earth were phrased to suit the format that the earth was static I.e. always the same size. After years and years of flawed theories to justify that concept, it was suddenly realized that the opposite was true. First of all, there was the plate tectonic theory that stated that the earth was of constant size and the continental plates moved around on the surface. After two generations, that theory was found to be flawed. There had to be some other theory to justify that the Atlantic was expanding. It was then that the subduction theory was presented. This theory stated that the pacific plate sub ducted under the North American and South American plate. Again, this was to justify a constant earth. The premise was that the Atlantic was known to be expanding; therefore, the Pacific had to be contracting. The contraction was effected by sub-duction under the Americas. Now, after another two generations of compiled data that theory was found to be flawed. The Pacific was also found to be expanding. GPS was overturning many previously accepted theories. I was showing up ancient shorelines all around the world with an unprecedented clarity. It was also telling us that these shorelines had reached higher elevations on land, much higher than ever before imagined. Not only was GPS showing up the flaws in current thinking as far as earth sciences gone. It was also showing that the history of civilization had to be rewritten. The information revealed would be of tremendous help to archaeologists, paleontologists, geologists, anthropologists and many other areas of science. With all the data collected and verified more startling discoveries started to emerge. What became abundantly clear was that many other theories about the earth and its surface were flawed. One such theory was Iostacy. It had been previously accepted that the earth rose from the sea because of a process called Isostatic Rebound. This propounded that the land mass rises from the sea because it has been relieved of the ice burden from the last ice age. The GPS survey had disproved all this. It had clearly shown that the sea receded from the land. This retreat of the sea created the illusion that the land mass rose. This theory was flawed because it had always been accepted that sea level was a fixed datum. Now that it was discovered that sea levels fell, and were always falling, the opposite appeared to be true. The exact mirror image of Isostatic Rebound is what was really happening. The sea levels were falling all around the world because of the earth's expansion. So, the conclusion was that Isostatic Rebound was an illusion caused by receding seas. Sea level was the variable factor in the equation: not a constant. This was really some momentous deduction, but what were they to do with the information? The amount of Information derived from the surveys was too much to handle at once. Too much of it was of a sensitive nature. A lid was put on all information. It had to be kept from the public domain. All the information was classified and a gag order was placed on all the agencies that had worked on GPS up to that point. All information and all future investigations were turned over to the National Optical Astronomy Observatory (NOAO). They were the only agency allowed to oversee and carry on research on the data, which had been compiled up to that time. All GPS maps, which had been made up to that time by the USGS, were classified. It was prohibited to sell any of the maps. All topographical maps that had been compiled with GPS sensitive information were classified for military purposes only. They could not be obtained on the open market. The Kyoto Protocol was initiated in 1997 and during the ensuing years the United States has become privy to all this information, which has influenced thinking about the earth and its mysteries. They know that Global Warming is a function of the earth's own internal heat. They also know that sea levels are falling all around the world. In the more than twenty years of the GPS development and data sea levels have dropped considerably. This drop in sea level far outstrips any rise forecasted by the Kyoto pronouncements. Now, they had also learned that Isostatic Rebound was an illusion and had no basis in reality. The United States is privy to all this information and this is one of the main reasons that they have withdrawn from signing the protocol.

Their decision not to sign has been met with harsh criticism by other member nations to the Kyoto Protocol. The Government of the United States will withstand this criticism in the name of what it knows and its own national security. Scientists and archaeologists, although not privy to any of this information, are chipping away at the truth. In more than one article archaeologists, in various parts of the world, are finding out what GPS has already revealed. There have been articles in the press about archaeological finds in high mountain areas, which will bring the secret into the open one way or another.

In the New York Times article "Civilization Cradle Grows Larger" Dr. Gill of Northwestern University has pointed out that a dig at Hamoukar indicates without a doubt that ancient civilization in Mesopotamia started higher up than previously thought. The Persian Gulf was much further inland at that time. GPS had revealed all this information. An article in the Times of Indian by Professors Gaur and Vora tells of finding ancient shorelines far inland at Gujarat. They have established that Gujarat was once a port on the Arabian Sea.

This article on the Kyoto Protocol opens up a whole lot of information about ancient sea levels and shorelines.

The modern day discoveries of the receding sea in New Jersey will bring other areas of the United States and the world. Other countries are already pouring over aerial photography of their shorelines to discover how much land has been left to them since ancient times.

Mesopotamia is termed the cradle of civilization and if the story of Noah is true there can be no doubt.

In ancient Mesopotamia the city of Nineveh was established by Noah, s grandson.

The town of Sandwich on the south coast of Britain had a large harbor in the middle Ages, today; however, the town is three miles inland. The Port of Ephesus in Turkey, where St. Paul landed on several occasions is now six miles inland. Ur of the Chaldees the birthplace of Abraham, the father of the Jewish Nation, was once a bustling port on the Persian Gulf. Today Ur is 200 miles from the sea and 135 feet above sea level. The most remarkable finding, however, and one that put a lid on a plethora of information is that Baghdad was also a port on the Gulf, ages ago, but is now 350 miles from the sea and 125 feet above sea level. All these anomalies have been confirmed by GPS and classified under a veil of national security. The maps and the information they contain have been classified. GPS and allied technology has revealed all the ancient shorelines around the world. It has also revealed much more than the Government is prepared to release. It has shown quite conclusively that sea levels were much higher in ancient times and as such dictated the development of civilization downward. It has given the United States advanced technological information, which it is reluctant to release for strategic purposes. The United States government is quite convinced that the sea levels will not rise worldwide. How do they know this? The answer lies in the data they have collected since the early days of GPS development. The fall in sea levels that they have detected clearly indicate that sea levels fall faster then any rise due to Global Warming. The Government now knows that any sea level rise will have a negligible effect on the already established recession of the seas. Is this the reason they will not sign the protocol? Not really, there is more. An article in the Wall Street Journal tells about a GPS survey revealing a sixty-foot boundary error between Rhode Island and Connecticut. This error corrected a survey done 140 years ago. GPS has shown up millions of such errors in surveys nationwide. If these errors were revealed it would tell us that not one piece of real estate is where it is supposed to be on the map. The very house you live in is not where it was last year. Your house lot has shifted and will keep shifting. If the extent of earth movement and coordinate shift were known it would create panic in the housing markets. Insurance Companies, Banks, Title and Mortgage companies would find themselves swamped in litigation. Let us just think for a moment. If the boundary of Rhode Island and Connecticut is out by 60 feet, what does that say for every boundary for every piece or parcel of land across the face of the United States? This is by no means the only problem. The Government cannot reveal that a mysterious growth of land across Texas is already causing territorial disputes between ranchers. All these newfound anomalies, and more, have to be kept under wraps by the Government. The fact that the earth is expanding will never be revealed for the same reason that the Government denies any UFO report. It does not want people to panic. What is a fact, however, is that the United States knows that our seas are receding and that Global Warming is caused by the Earth's own internal heat, which is increasing. GPS has provided them with this information. The Kyoto Protocol came into effect on February 16, 2005. The United States has become privy to much information, which bears directly on the tenets and articles of the Kyoto treaty. The two main precepts of the treaty are Global Warming and the resultant sea level rise. The United States has information, which refutes these concepts. We might never know the information, which GPS has revealed, through government channels. The United States will not reveal its information in defense of its refusal to sign. In the final analysis it is a matter of national security and that overrides all other national or international interests. The United States has said that it will not sign the protocol. The reason stated is that it will restrict national economic development. The truth, therefore, will only be revealed over time and through the most unlikely sources, as usual.

Archaeologists and other scientists all around the world will continue to whittle away at the veil of secrecy. They will do so within the parameters of their own professional pursuits. They will be going about business as usual. They will use facts, which they have at their disposal to make other discoveries. They will not, however, be in possession of information, which is currently classified. They will not be privy to all this wealth of information made available to us by GPS. They will, perhaps never know, that all they may discover in the future, through research and persistence, may be already known to the powers that be. The United States is in possession of knowledge and that knowledge translates into power. Australia, Croatia, Kazakhstan and Monaco have not signed as party to the Kyoto agreement and they all have their reasons for not signing. The United States has theirs. The official U.S. statement is that, to sign will interfere with economic progress in the years to come. We know better. Do we?

This article on the Kyoto Protocol reveals a lot of information about ancient sea levels and shorelines.

The modern day discoveries of the receding sea in New Jersey will bring other areas of the United States and the world into focus. Already, many other nations are pouring over aerial photography maps in an effort to uncover how much land has been left to them since ancient times.

When we consider how much information is being thrown at us today from various sources it is conceivable that a lot of this information is being classified: kept away from us for one reason or another. The amount of new information available is mind boggling. For one reason or another, governments find it necessary to classify information which they believe is not the best interest of their people, the public interest. Literally, translated this means: not in the government's interest.

In ancient Mesopotamia the city of Nineveh was established by Noah's grandson.

Mesopotamia is termed the cradle of civilization and if the story of Noah is true there can be little doubt. Iraq is the modern name for Mesopotamian which means between the rivers. The State of Iraq was set up by Winston Churchill in 1922 when he was Colonial Secretary of Britain. The book "Churchill's Folly" by Christopher Catherwood tells that story. I will relate the story of Noah and I hope it will reconcile what you have just read in the Kyoto Protocol article. You will be able to see that what is happening in New Jersey and New York is related to the story of Noah and the flood.

We all know that water seeks its own level. This is another anomaly that distorts the truth when it comes to sea level around the world. The seas are not level all around the surface of the earth and the variations in level are quite astounding considering that all the seas are interlinked. That is to say that the Pacific Joins the Atlantic at the bottom of South America and off the coast of Alaska Canada and Russia across the poles. The Atlantic Joins the Indian Ocean across the tip of South Africa and flows eventually to the Pacific Ocean further to Asia China and Japan and back to Russia. One would assume that because they are all interlinked that the sea levels would all be the same: that is not so. There are all sorts of influences on sea levels: some of these influences we know such as tides, currents, gravity and wind. There are others however we don't know about. These are sidereal and rotational influences that we are not even aware of that shape the seas and influence their levels. The sea is in a constant state of flux and as such immeasurable. We cannot determine true sea level for that is a fallacy: a myth. When we are told that sea levels are rising by two millimeters per annum we are being duped. We are being insulted. Our intelligence alone should tell us this. There is no effective measure of sea level known to man. All efforts have failed because there are too many variables in the seas equation. The Sea level on the Coast of Panama on the Pacific Ocean side is twenty two feet difference from the side on the Caribbean Sea. Yet the Pacific and Atlantic join at the tip of South America. So you see that there is the real difficulty in making any determination of sea level. We have been satisfied for centuries of maritime history to settle for a sea level referred to as Mean Sea Level. This is the mean between high and low tides. This mean is used in all countries to establish some means of reference for topographical levels on dry land. We use the term above mean sea level. Even that reference is nebulous for it is a mean between the tidal levels. The tides also play an integral part in the deception of sea level. We observe every day the tides coming in and going out. We know that as surely as they come in they will go out again.

We are able to compile tidal charts based on moon phases with great accuracy. As we watch the tides go in and out over the passage of time we are lulled into complacency.

Surely the tides come in and go out but over time we take the process for granted and look no further. What we fail to see is that the tides no longer come in as far as they did once upon a time. They have been creeping slowly away.

Why do we not observe the anomaly? The reason is that the tidal withdrawal takes place slowly over our lifetime. We don't have sufficient observational time to make a valid assessment. By which time we die and leave the earthly scene. Our son comes along and observes the tidal movement and assumes that his ancestors saw the same tidal movements. That however is not so. The son is seeing a different sea level from the one his forebears saw. The sea has withdrawn steadily and stealthily. This is the mystery behind receding seas. We don't live long enough to make valid observations of the seas withdrawal. Each successive generation comes along and accepts sea level as they see it. They are not aware of the recession. This is where aerial photography is proving a valuable tool in spanning the generation gap. The gradual withdrawal of the seas from shorelines around the world is caused by the earth's expansion. Each time there is an earthquake on land or under the sea the area of our planet increases and that increased surface are demands that the seas get shallower.

On the day after Christmas 2004 an earthquake erupted violently off the Island of Sumatra in Southeast Asia.

The earthquake caused a slump in the ocean floor which triggered a Tsunami. The Tidal wave swept through the Archipelago and reached as far as Sir Lanka and India.

Several lives were lost and millions in property damage.

The most interesting observation coming out of the aftermath is this. It has been reported that the sea has settled down again but it had withdrawn two hundred yards from its previous shoreline. Scientists have not seen the significance in this withdrawal.

I sat beside a lady on a flight recently and we spoke of many things including my books. I mentioned to her that the seas were receding. She was amazed for she became animated at the suggestion. In her own words she told me that she had sea front property in the Bronx and in New Jersey. She described how the houses on the Jersey shore all sit on a rise above the beach. There is a wide expanse of beach leading from the rise out to where the sea is at present. She went on to tell me that all that expanse of beach leading out to the seashore was once under water. She also told me that she had experienced the same anomaly in the Bronx. The lady worked in Lower Manhattan. What really convinced her was when I told her about Pearl Street.

Pearl Street in Manhattan was right on the East River three hundred years ago. Captain Kidd lived in a large house at the corner of Wall and Pearl Streets. Captain Kidd kept a small canoe on the east River in front of his house for commuting out to his ship which was moored in Brooklyn.

Now three hundred years later Pearl Street is 1800 feet from the East River and in between there is Water Street, Front Street, South Street and FDR Drive. This expansion of the city was made possible by the receding sea. As the foreshore gets shallow, because the sea recedes the city claims the land and makes use of it. This is happening along the Jersey shore where the Trump Taj Mahal was built on lands deserted by the sea. It is happening everywhere but as usual we fail to observe the subtlety. New York has also expanded on the West side. Broadway, three hundred years ago was on the Hudson River today however it is far removed from the river.

Burial grounds from the first century near Rome main airport are yielding a rare look into how ancient longshoremen and other manual workers did backbreaking jobs, archaeologists say.

The Necropolis which spanned the late first century into the second near the town of Ponte Galleria came to light last year when customs officers noticed a clandestine dig by grave robbers seeking valuable ancient artifacts.

Most of the 300 skeletons unearthed were male and many of them showed signs of years of heavy work; joint an tendon inflammation, compressed vertebrae, hernias and spinal problems were prevalent.

Judging from the condition of the skeletons it appeared that the men likely carried heavy loads in especially humid environment circumstances that makes one think of individuals who worked in the ports.

These findings by archaeologists are most interesting for the men worked at the port of Ostia fourteen miles from Rome. The Port was the main port for Rome in the Punic Wars.

All shipping came to Ostia and all the commodities were taken off the ships and loaded on to barges to be transported up the Tiber River to Rome. The loads were extremely heavy and the laborers had to do backbreaking work. There was a lot of activity at the port during the glory days of the Roman Empire.

The port of Ostia started silting up as the term is used and three successive emperors tried to keep it open with primitive methods of dredging. Well as you may imagine it was a Herculean task to keep dredging against a receding sea level. So finally Ostia was abandoned as the sea abandoned Ostia. Today Ostia is three miles from the sea. Ostia was established on the estuary of the Tiber but today the estuary of the Tiber is three miles from Ostia.

The other interesting not here is that all the laborers who worked at the port at Ostia and are buried in the grounds near the Rome Airport. The Airport is built on lands that were once part of Ostia. The lands that were once under the sea were claimed to build the airport. As time passes and the airport is expanded it will reach further and further out to claim more land from the sea as soon as the sea leaves it.

Many airports around the world are built on lands that were once under the sea. La Guardia and Kennedy airports were built on lands that were dumped up out of swamps surrounding New York. In 1942 the New York Port Authority dumped up one thousand acres of land in Jamaica Bay New York to create Idlewild airport. The airport opened in 1948. It was on this created Island in the middle of salt marshes. The salt marshes in Jamaica Bay at that time were extensive and the airport claimed one thousand acres.

When I first flew in and out of Idlewild airport in 1958 the salt marshes surrounded the airport. This could be seen clearly from the air. In subsequent years after the assassination of the President John F Kennedy the airport was renamed JFK in his honor and memory. Over the years on numerous landing and departures I have watched the dwindling salt marshes as the years passed. Now the EPA is concerned that the salt marshes are disappearing. The salt marshes have been disappearing gradually as the sea has receded. Today flying over Kennedy airport there are no more salt marshes to be seen they have all disappeared with the receding sea.

I try to put forward conclusive proof that our planet earth is expanding. I conclude that the expansion process makes seas recede from shorelines worldwide. Sea level datum is the misleading factor in the Isostatic Rebound theory. I state that "Both Sea Level Datum and Isostatic Rebound are myths: they do not exist.

The Mysterious Receding Seas

CHAPTER 5

An Article in the New York Times, Wednesday September 26th 2007 should put the matter of receding seas to rest once and for all. The title of the article is "JERSEY RIGHTS TO SHORE PROVE COSTLY TO CASINOS." Tells how the State of New Jersey is selling this land, left behind by the sea, to Casino Developers. It also tells how much land New Jersey has inherited from the sea since 1776. The State is selling and collecting taxes on these new lands. The "New Land" i.e. the land left behind by the receding sea is a worldwide phenomenon.

I stress that it is critical that science recognizes and accepts that our earth is expanding. In so doing we will solve many mysteries. We will understand why Salt Marshes and Wetlands disappear in the United States and around the world. We will understand why bridges over rivers fail mysteriously. We will know why all dams are threatened with failure. We will better understand what is happening to our rivers and why water resources are drying up. We will also understand why our earth is getting hotter, why our seas are getting hotter and why the Ice Caps is melting. We will understand why all ancient civilizations started in high regions of the world. We will also understand why so much land is becoming arid land. We will understand why Isostatic Rebound is flawed science. We will understand why storm and Hurricane intensity and Frequency are increasing. We will understand why New Orleans is sinking. We will understand why the Louisiana coastline is sinking. All river valleys are earthquake faults and we engineers built bridges and dams across them not aware of the fact that they all expand.

I show why early civilizations evolved in high mountains: that was the only land they had available in pre-history. I cite biblical references from Noah and the Ark to the Exodus showing how higher sea levels influenced these biblical events. All ancient civilizations evolved in high regions around the world. This fact, and the real reason, has never been addressed by historians. This is because sea level, through the ages, has always been accepted as a constant. On the contrary it is the variable in the earth expansion equation. Receding Seas reveal the flaw in the Isostatic Rebound Theory. Sea levels are not rising as the global warming proponents aver. The opposite is true and has been for a very long time: sea levels are falling.

Small nation states should be told the truth. I am Concerned that they will spend their scarces resources on an eventuality that will never occur. They must be told that sea levels will not rise and threaten their coastal security. They Must be told that the opposite is what is really happening. Small Island states need to know that media hype is feeding them with useless information.

Global warming is a fact of life. Our Earth is getting hotter no question. Why is our planet getting hotter? What causes the heat? Is it the burning of fossil fuels? Is it the build up of CO_2 in the atmosphere? Is it solar heat; is it methane emissions from rice paddies in China, or methane released by plants and animals generally? Could it be one or all of these sources or might it be something else?

Each time scientists create a theory the public accepts it. Why? Because we generally assume that scientists are specialists in their particular area of study. We therefore, regard their pronouncements as irrefutable. While that may be true it does not make them infallible. History has proven this and nowhere is this truer than in the Global Warming debate.

We have heard all sorts of reasons for climatic change brought about by Global Warming. We have heard about Global Warming with ever increasing intensity over the last few years. The Global Warming debate has reached fever pitch with the media and the scientific community pushing it down our throats. The intent obviously is to prevail upon a gullible public "to open wide and swallow" Make no mistake about it that is what we are supposed to do.

Over one hundred years ago scientists espoused the theory of Isostatic Rebound. The concept held that the land mass was rebounding from the sea. The theory was that the ending of the ice age relieved the land mass of the heavy ice burden and the land mass was now rebounding. Today it is recognized that the seas worldwide are, in reality, receding from shorelines. The evidence suggests that the sea levels have been receding constantly for thousands or millions of years. This on-going recession creates the illusion that the earth is rising. The delusion persists because of another of our established, but flawed, assumptions namely that sea level is a fixed datum. Nothing could be further from the truth as we will see.

The Isostatic Rebound theory was invalid from the start. There was no such thing. The scientific deductions were wrong. But for over one hundred years that was the prevailing argument and we swallowed it.

So now that we know that sea levels are receding we are being told by scientists that the sea levels are rising. Another argument prevailing is that sea level is so unstable that it cannot possibly be determined. So what are we to believe?

After all this scientists tell us that because of Global Warming sea level is rising two millimeters per year. Are we really supposed to believe that? Two millimeters is the difference between the improbable and inane. For scientists to tell us that is an insult to our collective intelligence. It is time that we take a serious look at what we are being told and what we are supposed to believe. We have to ask ourselves what makes scientists miss clues about our earth's behavior. The answer is simply that the earth is deceptive in her behavior and scientists misinterpret her behavior.

After all we are only human, and even scientists are apt to err. The damage is that these misconceptions, over time, become dangerous dogma too deeply entrenched to be easily erased. They steer, direct us often away from, and obscure the truth which I find disconcerting.

When scientists conceive new concepts: They apply for grants to do research on their theories. Grants, the life blood of scientific research, are often difficult to get. Once obtained the scientist is obligated to publish and produce positive results. Scientists are loath to jeopardize their chances of securing future grants by compromising their or their institutions reputation. No scientist will get up and say he was wrong and lose his grant: and in so doing lose face. He will defend his theory until he dies. The sad thing is that his theories if they are wrong do not die with him but goes on to mislead other generation. Sometimes the scientist in defending his theory is really defending his grant: it's a thin line.

So in the Global Warming Debate what are we to believe: Let's see.

When the first Trans Atlantic cable was laid on the ocean floor in 1857 the cables kept snapping. The cables had to be dragged and grappled from the Ocean floor, one mile down, and repaired. As soon as they were repaired and dropped back on the ocean floor they broke again. What was the cause of these recurring breaks in the cables? For one hundred years scientists proposed to the public and investors alike that undersea landslides and undersea turbidity currents were responsible for the cable failures. That's what we were told then and that's what we believed for one hundred years as the cables kept snapping.

In 1959 the mid Atlantic rift was discovered. The mid Atlantic ridge is formed by two mountain ranges running north to south in the Atlantic Ocean. The mountain ranges run parallel to each other, one mile apart. What had been happening was that the small communication cables were spanning the one mile gap in between these mountains. They were spanning a mile. The cables were never designed for the stresses that such a span would impose: so they kept snapping. After one hundred years, it was discovered why the cables snapped and kept snapping. The Scientists were just as ignorant as all of us. Everyone back then thought that the ocean floor was flat and sandy. Scientists came up with the theory of undersea landslides and Turbidity currents and we swallowed it for one hundred years. The most interesting outcome of all this is that since the mystery of the snapping cables was solved back in 1959 nothing more was ever heard of turbidity currents and undersea landslides. Nothing like that ever existed.

Science Research and Scientists are funded by corporations and endowment funds. What we have to define is who says what and when: Scientists get grants to do research and in order to keep these grant funds coming they keep feeding the media with sensational tit bits. The media in turn publishes these tit bits in order to keep the public awareness up. The public has to be scared and kept scared for the funds to keep coming.

Remember the killer bees scare a generation ago. A ferocious variety of killer bees from Africa had crossed the Atlantic to South America. There they interbred with local varieties to create a killer bee. Each successive year the bees kept coming closer to the United States. Scientists were given grant funds to study the killer bees. Every year there was news that they were getting closer to the US border. They eventually came into Mexico and again the media scared the daylights out of people. The media scare came every year, on schedule, when their grant funds were due for renewal.

Forty years ago scientists came up with the Plate Tectonic Theory. All the continents plates they said floated around on the viscous mantle in the earth. That Theory was accepted for a generation until the flaws begun to appear. Yes: the plates did move: computers could show that very clearly. However, the sum of all the parts did not add up to the whole. There were missing piece in the jig saw puzzle. It appeared that the earth was expanding. This could definitely not be so because our earth is of a constant size. We must all accept that the earth is of constant size because that is entrenched dogma.

Our Planet Earth is supposed to be of a constant size. That is what we are taught and that is what we are supposed to believe.

So everything to do with earth anomalies is rationalized to suit an earth of constant size.

In 1959 we discovered that the mid Atlantic ridge was pushing North America away from Europe by about six feet every sixty years. The Atlantic was getting wider. If the earth was of a constant size it would necessarily follow that the Pacific must be contracting to accommodate the expansion of the Atlantic.

A generation later however, it was discovered that the Pacific was also expanding. That was an inconvenient truth. Something had to be done to get the earth back in shape. So what did science do?

They came up with the subduction theory which proposed that the pacific sea floor is being tucked away underneath the North American continent. This makes for a tidy earth of constant size. We simply tuck the Pacific sea floor under North America and presto no problem; the earth remains the same size.

Now as preposterous as this may seem this is what Scientists proposed to suit the constant earth hypothesis. That is what they told us and that is what we were supposed to believe. This against all other indications that our earth was expanding now after another generation had gone by subduction is found to be a flawed theory. It is now realized that the earth is expanding. That is the way science misleads us. They come up with theories and we are supposed to close our eyes, open wide and swallow.

Global Warming is no different we are being bombarded with facts, figures and graphs and we must swallow without thinking. Are we about to mislead another generation? The earth on which we live holds many secrets. We know very little about her the earth does not impart her secrets readily. She is mysterious. Her behavior is enigmatic and scientists misinterpret this behavior and compile flawed theories. And so it is with global Warming After one hundred years of erroneous theories it is time we started thinking and suss things out for ourselves. It's not as difficult as it sounds. Today we have the internet and the wealth of information it provides. Today we can find out everything for ourselves. As I say the earth is getting hotter but the big question is why? What is the real cause of Global Warming? We all overlook the earth's internal heat? As the earth expands it radiates more heat. NASA thermal maps of the world show us clearly how the earths land and sea temperatures have heightened over the last fifty years.

The Tsunami that swept over Southeast Asia on Boxing Day 2004 caused extensive damage and loss of life. The Tsunami was caused by a massive earthquake off the Island of Sumatra. The Earthquake caused the ocean floor to slump causing the massive tsunami. The result we all know for reports of the tragedy captured headlines for a sustained period. The effects of the Tsunami will be felt for a long time by the Inhabitants as they seek to regain their peaceful existence from the chaos. The sea has settled down again off the coast of Southeast Asia but a subtle difference has been noted by the inhabitants. . Scientists, however, have not noticed, or for that matter, taken any notice of this most important anomaly. Surely the sea had settled down again on the coast and once more laps the shoreline in gentle successive waves. The only difference is that it has not returned to its former level on the shore. It has receded and the level of the sea had dropped considerably. This is all caused by the slump in the ocean floor that caused that massive upheaval. The sea has receded in the aftermath; this anomaly is never noted for its significance. Its importance to earth sciences is totally overlooked. This phenomenon is what I am alluding to. The mysterious departure of the seas: the recession process. The recession is all part of the earth expansion phenomenon. Earthquakes trigger the expansion process and that phenomenon in turn triggers the recession process. It is a subtle recession for the most part but sometimes it is more violent. Darwin would have seen this anomaly as a raised beach. The opposite is true.

In a major earthquake in Nicaragua some years ago the sea retreated and dropped twenty feet in level offshore. Although it was observed and reported the significance was lost. Nothing is known about the process of recession and the causes of the phenomenon.

In April 2007 a seismic jolt unleashed the deadly Solomon's Tsunami. It lifted an entire Island meters out of the sea destroying some of the worlds most pristine coral reefs.

In an instant the grinding of the earths tectonic plates forced the island upwards by three meters.

Submerged reefs that once attracted scuba divers from around the globe lie exposed and dying after the quake raised the mountainous mass.

The stench of rotting fish and other marine life stranded on the reefs when the sea receded is overwhelming and the once vibrant coral reef is dry and crunches underfoot.

Dazed villagers stand on the shoreline still trying to come to terms with the cataclysmic shift that changed their geography of their island forever. Pushing the shoreline out to sea by up to two hundred feet.

The islands harbor has disappeared leaving only a narrow inlet filled with exposed jagged reefs on either side.

The inhabitants report large fissures splitting the Island in half some are eighteen inches wide

Scuba divers report that a large chasm has opened up offshore running parallel to the coast. Sunken vessels from the pacific war have been exposed on the sea floor.

The villagers fear that the sea will come back again and they are reluctant to come down from higher ground.

The reports coming back from other areas of the Solomon's is that the coral damage has been widespread with the exposure of reefs above the receding sea level

After the great earthquake in Lisbon in 1773 it was reported that the sea receded leaving boats aground on the sea floor. The sea never returned to its former level.

The subtle departure of the sea is not noticed in most cases. The cases I have sited here is just to show that if the earthquake is massive it will make drastic changes in sea level. The drop in level is noted in one location that has been affected but in other remote regions the sea had also retreated but not noticed, The large shocks that create drastic sea level drops is easily recognized as being part of the earthquake aftermath, But further away from the epicenter the sea is also receding as a result of that remote earthquake. The departure is more subtle and goes unnoticed. In the case of the Solomon's earthquake the far flung areas of the Islands all reported that the sea had exposed their reefs and ruined them by exposing them to direct sunlight.

The earthquake shock was massive enough to bring all these recessions into focus but that is the end of it. The recession of the sea is viewed in isolation, it was caused by the earthquake and that is that. The cognitive connection is not made between the earthquake and the fissures on the shore and on the sea and the retreat of the sea. All these anomalies are viewed as separate and isolated. There is no cognizance of the fissures on shore and offshore being related to the receding seas and the exposure of the reefs, this ignorance goes on constantly. The slump in the ocean floor is never mentioned again as a contributing factor the the seas recession.

In the case of the 2004 Tsunami the receding sea is not viewed it he larger context. The slump on the ocean floor is one isolated point. The Tsunami is another and the earthquake is another there is no relationship to the fact that after the tsunami the sea does not return to its former level on the shoreline. The phenomenon are all related

It is significant that shorelines around the world recede over the ages. Nowhere is the anomaly more noticeable that around the Mediterranean and more specifically around the shores of the Aegean Sea. All the ancient cities that feature in history Mycenae, Troy Ephesus and Ramsees are all six miles inland today. This anomaly points to a steady recession of the sea in that area. The Mediterranean is landlocked and so is the Aegean so it is a typical encapsulation of the seas recession. It is even more pointed that over on the Mediterranean shore of Egypt the city of Ramsees was discovered six miles inland in 1883.

Winston Churchill in his book' The History of the English Speaking Peoples" tells how Britain separated from France millions of years ago. The Rhine used to flow across Britain and had its estuary in the Irish Sea. He tells how the White Cliffs of Dover match the cliffs on the French side of the Channel. If the land masses were to close again the cliffs would match perfectly where they once sundered to use Churchill's word. He relates how trawlers that drag the channel pull up from time to time the roots of the ancient Oaks that grew where the Channel is now. Britain has about four earthquakes per year and the epicenter is usually in the middle of the English Channel where the separation is taking place. This is also where the Chunnel crosses from Britain to the Continent.

The authors suspicion `of the earths behavioral patterns grew out of his engineering practice... With the passing years he noticed several contradictory anomalies that aroused his interest. They defied explanation and so he started to take a closer look at the earth and her movements. He was amazed to discover how deceptive the earth as. In the first case he had always had a curious mind which he inherited from his father. He found out that we are constantly being deceived by what the earth is showing us compared with what we are taught in institutions of learning. The earth is able to mislead us because of what we are taught and how we interpret her behavior. Most of what we are taught he discovered to be wrong. We however tend to continue along paths of what we are taught. Therein lies the continued deception. We are lead further and further away from the truth. We weave all sort of fantastic concepts and theories to justify the deception and come up with more questions than answers. We have to start thinking for ourselves. We have to open our minds and flush them of all that we have learned about our earth and start all over again. We have been living on the earth for millions of years and we still know nothing about terra firma except that it is not so firm. The earth goes about its process of expansion it is not hiding anything from us. The problem is that we make the wrong observations and build theories on those erroneous observations. Later someone else comes along and builds more theories on these erroneous theories and the clouds descend. We all wonder around in a cloud of deception all based on false premises.

When an earthquake occurs or when a volcano spurts lava we take only momentary notice of these events and go one with our daily lives. It is only if our lives are disrupted by a major earthquake or volcano do we feel our lives affected. That is when we take notice. So it is with many other events and activities in life. If it impacts on you individually it gets your attention. Otherwise we take it all for granted and go on with the pursuit of our own lives. We never take an earthquake or a volcano as a part of the global expansion process. Earthquakes occur every second of every day somewhere on the face of our earth. All these earthquakes leave fissures which add dimension to the earth's surface. We don't know this and we really don't care unless it affects us personally. Earthquakes and expansion is however going on all the time every moment every minute every hour and every day of every year.

When you fly over the great United States you can see for yourself all the ancient lava flows that crisscrossed the continent millions of years ago. In some locations the topography is altered by as much as a mile in height like the Snake River Canyon. The Snake River cuts through a lava bed One mile thick. All these abnormalities can be seen from an aircraft flying miles above the earth. The earth's features rifts and faults can be seen quite easily from those heights. As a matter of fact the entire tectonic maps imagery came out of the age of satellites. Satellites showed us how the earth as fractured and shaped by tectonic action. We were able to see for the first time how lacerated and striated the surface of the earth was with earthquake faulting. We always think that earthquakes occur elsewhere and not in our locality. That is of course if it does. When however it occurs in our city we sit up and take notice but only temporarily. We were all surprised when Mt St Helens erupted years ago and wreaked so much havoc. Because the United States is so large it appeared to many of us remote. Yet to the people in the area it was a wake up call because their lives were directly affected.

We did not however know that elsewhere around the world other volcanoes were erupting and pumping inestimable amounts of lava out on the earth's surface.

We are creatures of locality and insulated by events that occur elsewhere. We also live on a large continent not on some small island like Montserrat where a volcano makes it necessary to evacuate our homeland. Millions of years ago there have been some massive volcanoes here in the United States. As you drive across the land you can still see remnants of them. Someday they may become active again. Driving through Nevada in the Lake Tahoe and Reno areas you can observe the smoke rising from the ground as you pass by. Who knows when these areas will blow up and erupt into a volcano?

Some years ago a farmer in Mexico saw a small bump rise up in his cornfield and over a period of time it grew larger and larger until it blew into a major volcano. Every time the earth quakes it is relieving built up tension. That tensional release created fissures and those fissures add up across the surface of the earth.

I have often been asked how I account for the expansion of the earth if the earth is of a finite amount of material. The explanation is simply this. The lava that is pumped out on the surface of the earth comes from the molten interior rock of the earth. The lava is being pumped out under extreme pressure. It eventually blows out of the earth under this intense internal pressure. The rock immediately begins to cool and as it is expended it also expands to many times it original size in the earth. As it cools it loses its density and becomes pumice but in the process of cooling the volume increases. It expands as it cools giving the earth crust its density which is much lighter than the interior density for the earth but it has also expanded to many times its original volume in the earth. The earth itself has expanded to as much as twice its original size. The earth was once the size of the Moon 2000 miles across but today it is 7800 miles across. Earthquakes leave their trademark crack all over the landscape. In California you can see cracks that are actually moving as you observe the, these can also be seen on the coast of Louisiana. Fault lines move constantly although for the most part we can't observe the movement. All river valleys are earthquake faults and we as engineers build dams and bridges across them without even being aware that these faults are expanding. In recent time I am happy to say the bridge authorities have been retrofitting bridges for earthquakes because many bridges have failed mysteriously because of this seismic creep phenomenon. I drove a bridge on the Mississippi years ago and sometime later I read where the bridge had failed and fallen into the Mississippi. Also the failure of the Minnesota Bridge could also be contributed to the expansion of the Mississippi River fault line. The configuration of the twisted gusset plates indicate that longitudinal stresses could have caused the failure of the bridge. The Mississippi is a known earthquake fault and is constantly expanding. Engineers should pay attention to any design over any river and allow for expansion.

When I say that all river valleys are earthquake faults I mean all over the world. They are all open wounds on the earth's surface. They were all caused by earthquake action and they all expand from time to time. It is a sweeping statement and meant as a sweeping connotation. We must also remember that there are millions of fault lines all around the world. We must not lose sight of the fact that the earth is covered with water. The surface of the water covering the earth comprised 70% of the surface of the earth. The exposed land area is 30% and growing. The earthquake activity under the ocean is just as active as the action on land and its going on constantly day after day. This simply means that the surface of the earth under the oceans is also expanding and the water cover is the same by volume. This increase in land surface must dictate that sea levels change; get shallower to spread itself thinner to cover the increased land area. So we must not lose sight of that fact, the earth is expanding under the seas as well as on land. The ratio of expansion of land under the sea to dry land is 70% to 30%. The greater land expansion is taking place under the sea. Tectonic maps are now available for all countries over the earth. Certain maps are classified especially with the war in Iraq. But it is quite possible to purchase these maps from the USGS offices.

Sometime ago I was consulted to design an 800 Million Gallon Reservoir. The reservoir was to be attached to a reservoir that had been built years before the age of satellites. In doing my soil investigations in the area I bought tectonic maps and studied them. The tectonic map showed that the old reservoir was built on an earthquake fault. In doing further research I found out a lot of information about the original reservoir. The interesting point is that the fault ran through the reservoir but it only showed the fault line going in to the reservoir and coming out the other side. But the reservoir hid the fault from the satellite because the Reservoir was filled with water when the satellite took the photographs. The other thing I learned was that after the reservoir was completed back in 1948 it was being filled for the first time when an earthquake occurred. The earthquake tore a two inch wide fissure in the side of the reservoir twenty feet below the water line. The fissure emptied the reservoir down to the fissure line in three days. The fissure line was ten feet above the bottom of the reservoir. This fact alarmed me for no one knew about this occurrence: it had happened fifty years before. The reservoir was thirty feet deep. It would be a major catastrophe if such an earthquake would occur again when the city was now tripled in size. The city would be without water. The new reservoir was required because the old one had silted up to the ten foot level. This meant that only twenty feet of water was retained at any one time when the reservoir was full. If the fissure was to reopen now the reservoir would be totally empty in three days. Having done all my geothermal research and written the feasibility report I presented it to my clients and made an oral presentation to all the executives who were the decision makers.

I pointed out all that I had found. They then asked me if we could locate the new reservoir somewhere where there was no fault. I made them aware of the fact that anywhere they located the reservoir would still be sitting on a fault. It was then decided to build the reservoir over the same fault but with certain advanced techniques that would be failsafe in case of another earthquake.

Many dams built across the United States and the world are failing slowly because of the same seismic movement and expansion of fault lines. The Bolder and Glen Canyon Dams all leak around the abutments as the river fault expands.

At this time the reader should be able to see how the earth fools us with her receding seas. We should also be able to see how we are lead by the receding seas. You should also see how we cover up the evidence by utilizing the land as soon as it becomes available from the sea. All around the world new structures are being built on lands that have been deserted by the sea. We are not able to encompass what has taken place before we came along we just accept things as we see them. We also accept the sea where we see it. We assume naturally that the sea has always been at the level we observe. This is not so this is how we are deceived from generation to generation. This is our earth at her elusive best. Because of the lack of awareness in successive generations we miss the point of recession. As cities grow and burst at the seams it is inevitable that we build roads along our waterfronts. That is the only land we have available on an ongoing basis as a city expands. That is why Chicago has it lakeshore drive: Manhattan it,s west side highway and on the east side the FDR highway. These are the only new areas of land that can be found consistently. And so it goes on this process of expansion. Three hundred years ago Pearl Street was on the East River. As the City expanded Water street was added. Later front street was added and later FDR. All this expansion has taken place just because it was made possible as the sea receded. The same development trend is noted in Wales on the Southeastern end of Britain. Some years ago I noted that all the Roman Roads built in Wales were inland. I learned that they were built originally on the seacoast. They were all now inland and far away from the sea. We built an Oil Refinery in Milford Haven, Wales sometime in the sixties. The land on which it was erected was under the sea years before.

I have been very fortunate to have visited several seaside locations in the course of my engineering work and so was able to make these observations. The earth uses her timelessness to avoid detection. The earth has been performing her magic act for million of years. We its inhabitants are not aware that we have been following the sea for as long as we have had civilization.

So far we have only scratched the surface of our research about the earth and her behavioral patterns. She still defies us and leads us on. In the last hundred years we have learned a lot but we still know nothing it we were to plot our progress on a graph. The sad conclusion is that we still know very little. One of the main problems is that we are being taught the wrong things and we keep following erroneous concepts. The earth is still having the last laugh. It is literally impossible to talk to any professor of geology about earth expansion although the facts are staring him in the face. He had to stick to an established curriculum. There is no deviating from that... Some years ago I spoke to geologists. I asked him the pointed question: Would earth expansion solve a lot of the problems that now perplex geologists?. He answered in the affirmative. It would solve so many geological puzzles. It would also solve many Archaeological puzzles. It would also solve a host of

Palaeontological problems and of course it would solve a lot of Earth Science puzzles. Taken over all it would open up fresh new avenues of scientific exploration. We would bring about a renaissance in science. I can hardly wait to see what will transpire when we eventually arrive at the conclusion that our seas are receding.

We discovered the mid Atlantic rift in the middle of the last century and we have been exploring the ocean depths since then with submersibles. We have learned very little. We still are finding more and more anomalies as time goes on. Just a year ago Geologists from Bristol University set sail for the mid Atlantic to find out what is going on. They discovered a large wound in the earth's surface that opened up the earth down to the very mantle. The results of their research still have to be known. In the final analysis if we find that the seas are receding we will have no other avenue of truth but that our earth is expanding. If we find that the earth is expanding we have to allow that the seas must recede. The one hinges on the other and the two in collusion will lead us to the truth.

New concepts will have to come to the forefront we can keep hammering the old and the outdated concepts. Most of the hypotheses that we have been taught are wrong. They need to be revised and or re examined. Science needs a breakthrough as far as earth expansion and receding seas go. We cannot continue to stumble on in darkness. Our earth is a miracle of creation just as we are. Let us spend sometime to find out about her so that when we leave her for eternity we can say that we have solved some of her secrets and given a breath of fresh air to scientific endeavor.

Einstein said that all things in the universe are relative; by this he meant related. We know that the Sun is expanding. We know that the other planets are expanding we know that the Universe is expanding; Why not the earth: all things being relative?

Albert Einstein.